Seren and the
Polar Bear Cub
by Sadie Jones

To Mam and Dad,
my inspiration every day.

Author Bio

Photo of Sadie in Longyearbyen, Svalbard in January 2020.

Dr Sadie Jones is the Astronomy Public Engagement Leader at the University of Southampton. She completed her PhD in black hole astrophysics in 2011 and since then has worked on delivering an exciting program of astronomy outreach activities. She has designed several creative astronomy projects to engage both children and adults with the university's astronomy research, such as the AstroAirport, Aurora Art and Black Hole Poetry projects.

In January 2020, she accompanied the Space Environment Physics (SEP) group on an expedition to Svalbard, Norway to launch their Aurora Zoo citizen science project (aurorazoo.org). After seeing the aurora for the first time on that trip and having a real-life encounter with a polar bear Sadie became inspired to write a book all about her adventure for the children who attend her aurora workshops. She now also works on 'Astronomy Voyage' cruises in and around Norway every year, delivering lectures on astronomy research and sharing her new love of the aurora with tourists from around the world.

This is her first novel.

Chapter 1

"Would you like to come on a spacewalk with me, Bili?" Seren quizzes her small white and fluffy cavachon dog, as she scratches his belly. As usual, Seren's mind is wandering, she's imagining that she's an astronaut gliding around in space, just chilling out, looking at the stars in between her important work on the space station. Daydreaming happens most of the day in Seren's overactive mind. She's ten-years-old, but ever since the age of five, when the UK astronaut Tim Peake came to her school, she says confidently, to anyone who will listen, "I want to be an astronaut when I grow up!"

Today is the last day of the Christmas holidays for Welsh schools, and the reality is that Seren isn't an astronaut working for the European Space Agency exploring the edge of space. Instead, she is lying on her belly in her living room, wearing her favourite purple dungarees and yellow, star-themed t-shirt, stroking Bili dog and flicking her legs behind her with much speed. As her mind wanders further, she pretends that she has become untethered from the space station and that she is floating through the purply-pink hydrogen gas in the Orion Nebula – this is her favourite floor activity.

Suddenly a loud snuffling comes from the sofa, snapping Seren away from her space adventure and back to reality. The reality is that it's one o'clock in the afternoon on a not so special, grey and rainy day in the valleys of South Wales. The snuffling is her dad, Garry, snoring away on his lunch break. Seren's dad works for the Welsh Apprentices Program (WAP), he links up with businesses across Wales and helps support them so they can take on young apprentices, at the moment he is working with an engineering company. All his work is online these days, so when he's not in the dining room at his stand-up desk talking about important WAP stuff, he can be found napping on the sofa with Bili. "Wake up, Dad! I'm soooo bored, let's take Bili for a walk, shall we?" Seren shouts into her dad's face. As Seren's dad stirs from his slumber, he doesn't reply to his daughter's idea but instead he reaches for the TV remote next to him on the settee and looks at his watch.

"Is that the time? I haven't even seen the news today, Seren!"

It's impressive how often Seren's parents watch the news; 9am, 1pm, 6pm, they even watch it at 10pm after Seren goes to bed. Seren hates watching the news. It's so depressing. In fact, she doesn't watch much TV at all because she finds it so hard to sit and focus. She's very easily distracted. If the show is about space, then she can concentrate no problem. Her friends like to play a game at school called 'Spacewalk' where they all pretend to be astronauts fixing the International Space Station, but some of the other girls get annoyed with Seren because she keeps correcting them when they don't use the proper words for things – Seren says things like "this game should be called 'EVA' not 'Spacewalk', EVA stands for Extra Vehicular Activity."

Seren used to get told off a lot at school for daydreaming and her inability to focus on tasks. However, her mother got her an appointment online with a nice doctor named Dr Sally who told Seren that she was neurodiverse, and this is why she struggles to focus on tasks she considers boring. Seren isn't entirely sure what being neurodiverse means, but her mam, Stella, said it means her brain works differently so sometimes she experiences the world differently from most people. But these differences aren't a bad thing! They're likely part of the reason that Seren is so creative and has such an amazing and active imagination. Sometimes Seren might need some extra help with her schoolwork which can be hard for her because she's a perfectionist who doesn't like asking for help, and her mam says her ADHD is why she's very sensitive and gets easily upset sometimes, especially if she thinks the children in school are leaving her out of games. It also the reason why she gets really stressed when there are sudden loud sounds (usually hand dryers), and she can't wear certain clothes (anything with a high neck or with the label still on).

When Seren is really interested in something, she can focus on it incredibly well. Seren's Dad calls her 'in-the-zone' when this happens. Sometimes he gets annoyed with her when she is 'in-the-zone' because she can't hear him calling upstairs to ask if she wants a cup of tea and he ends up shouting it three times and stamping his feet before she finally answers him. The answer is always "yes please Dad!" While 'in-the-zone', Seren can sit mesmerised learning about anything to do with space and astronomy, her current hyperfocus is doing colourful drawings of black holes with their bright discs and their long spinning jets. She can even watch her favourite TV show 'Space Sisters' for hours non-stop (see even forgets to go to wee sometimes), but just one minute of trying to focus on the news is enough to make her very stressed and anxious.

Despite Seren's strong dislike for both the news and loud sounds, Garry turns up the volume of the TV to a deafening level. She hears her local bespectacled news reader, June Bevan, declare, "Breaking News, people across the whole of the UK including Wales should look North into the night sky from 6 o'clock tonight. If you are lucky, and the sky is clear you might be able to see the wonderful green and red lights of the aurora dancing across the sky." Seren jumps up from the floor and stands in front of her dad, blocking his view of the TV.

"Dad, you lied to me, you told me the only place you could see the aurora was in the Arctic Circle, like in Lapland. That news lady just said you can see it from Wales!" says Seren angrily eyeing her father.

"I didn't lie to you Seren, I honestly thought that you had to go really far north to see the aurora, but this is great, don't you see? Me and your mam don't have to take you to Lapland now, you can see the Northern Lights from our garden, tonight!" he smirks at her cheekily.

Seren jumps up and down on the spot, her blonde curls bouncing into her face. "I can't believe I am going to see the Northern Lights in South Wales. This is so cool!" Seren darts away from her dad and goes straight to the cupboard under the stairs to put on her coat and trainers, Bili is following her because he thinks it's walkies time. "Seren, it's only twenty minutes past one, we have another five hours before it gets dark enough for us to see it!" Her Dad shouts in dismay.

Seren flops dramatically to the floor in the hallway with half of her body inside her coat as Bili licks her face "Blerfgh Bili! Ger off me...What am I going to do for five whole hours Dad? I'm so bored!"

"I know," says Garry. "How about you use your laptop to do some research on the Northern Lights and try and understand what is happening to make them visible in the UK. That will keep you busy for a bit, and I can watch the rest of the news in peace!"

Seren heads to her bedroom, which is space themed, of course, and starts to Google things like 'Aurora in Wales' and 'Northern lights in the UK'. The webpages are either really complicated with lots of words she doesn't understand, or they just have pretty photos of aurora but with no explanation of what causes them to be visible so far south, like here in the UK.

Seren is about to give up hope and throw her laptop on the floor again. She has done this several times before because she has very little patience, but then she sees in the search listing an interesting looking website called 'The Aurora Zoo citizen science project'. She clicks on the link, and it opens onto a black and green coloured page with words like 'Research' and 'Classify' on.

Seren starts with the 'About' section. The website explains that the 'Aurora Zoo' is project led by aurora scientists at the University of Southampton in South England. The project uses a special camera to take photos of the aurora and the space scientists, who work in Southampton mostly, have put the camera in a place called Svalbard in Norway. Seren goes on to read more about the 'Team Members' for the project and one of them is called Dr Julie Owen, which Seren assumes, based on their surname, means that she is Welsh like her, so that's cool!

Dr Owen is wearing a big purple puffer coat in her profile photo, with a big white telescope dome in the background. Seren instantly thinks Dr Owen is going to be a very cool person because Seren also has a purple puffer coat that looks very similar. The website says that Dr Owen's job title is 'Astronomy Outreach Leader'. Seren isn't sure what 'Outreach' is but as she reads the description it becomes clear that Dr Owen's job involves explaining astronomy and the science of the aurora to the public and to young children like Seren. Below the profile photo of Dr Julie Owen is her email address. Seren calls down the stairs, "Dad, can I email this Welsh scientist in Southampton to ask her about why the Northern Lights are visible tonight in Wales?"

Garry shouts back over the sound of the news broadcast, "Yes, I'm sure that will be fine just copy me into the email too Seren, ok?"

"Ok Dad," she replies.

Seren frantically types up her email to Dr Owen, stopping only to gaze out of her window a moment to look at a single white cloud that hangs over the lush green mountains.

As she clicks on 'Send' and leans back in her purple desk chair, Bili nuzzles his head into her leg, looking up at her with his massive eyes. "Hopefully she will reply to me quickly, Bili. I really want to understand how it's possible to see the Aurora from Wales!" she says as she ruffles Bili's head fur with her hand.

"What's the Aurora?" replies Bili.

Chapter 2

So yeah, Seren can sometimes hear Bili's thoughts in her mind when she touches his head. She's been able to do it since she was seven years old. The first time she discovered it was by accident. Bili was very ill. She had a strong feeling whenever she consoled him with a head massage that Bili had a pain in his tummy. It's not like she hears actual sound coming from his mouth. That would be ridiculous! But sometimes it's like she knows exactly what he is thinking. Bili isn't a particularly smart dog though, so often the strong thoughts that Seren feels when she touches his head are things like 'Ball, Ball, Ball', 'Beach' or 'I really want cheese!' It's quite shocking that for once the thoughts getting through to Seren are something more serious and less... dog? It seems even Bili is captivated by the science of the aurora.

Luckily, Seren already has a pretty good understanding of aurora science, so turning away from the window, she moves off the swivel chair and onto the floor with Bili. She rests her hand back on top of his fluffy head and starts to speak out loud.

"Well, Bili, it's this amazing natural light display that happens high up in the atmosphere; it's to do with the Sun." She pauses, and checks that Bili seems to be following. His big dark eyes gaze back at her with interest, so she continues.

"The Sun gives out light, as you know, because you can see it in the daytime when we go on our walks. The Sun also shoots out this other stuff called *particles,* the scientists call this the 'solar wind'. Sometimes these particles from the Sun make it to the Earth's atmosphere; the atmosphere is all around the Earth, and it's made of air. You can't see the air with your eyes though. Anyway, the Sun particles have lots of energy and they are suddenly colliding with the air. Now, one of the gases in air is called oxygen. It's very good that there is so much oxygen in the air because humans and dogs, we need it to breathe. Well, this oxygen gets excited, what I mean by 'excited' is that the oxygen gas will now have more energy because the Sun particles smashed into it very fast. So, the oxygen will be given some of the Sun's energy, which means the oxygen lights up and glows. Different gases in the atmosphere around the Earth glow different colours. It's a bit like how you see different colours in the fireworks by the seaside when we watch them every November in Porthcawl, but I know you don't like fireworks." Seren stops momentarily to take a breath because she has been speaking faster than usual, and Bili isn't the smartest of dogs, so it is probably best he has time to think about all this new information.

"Now, these Sun particles only come into to the top and bottom of Earth's atmosphere, close to the poles. We don't usually see it here in Wales because we are too far south on the Earth." Seren pauses and gives Bili a treat from her stash on her desk because he is being such a good boy and listening so well.

"Most of the time, the aurora that people see is green or red in colour, and that's because of the oxygen gas glowing. It can actually glow two colours at the same time, but the green aurora is more common. I don't know about dogs, but because of the way our eyes work us humans can see the green aurora more easily than the red." Seren says, stroking from Bili's head all the way down to the fur on his back. She then strokes her hand back up onto his head.

"I don't know if you remember, but Mam and Dad said they would take me to Lapland before I go to big school so that I can see the aurora because I've been obsessed with seeing it ever since I read a book about it when I was eight. Lapland is really far North; they have lots of snow there. But now Dad says we won't need to go to Lapland if we are able to see it tonight. But I don't mind Bili, because it would be so cool to see it from Wales, all the photos of it online are so beautiful. It would be aaaammmmmaaaziinnng!"

Once Seren is quiet from overspilling aurora facts from her young brain, she puts her hand once again onto Bili's oh so fluffy head. At first, she can't sense any thoughts coming from him. She's about to give up and move her hand away and get back up into her chair, but there it is, just a tickle in her mind, "I do hope we can see it tonight, Seren."

"Me too Bili, me too," Seren responds as she climbs back onto her purple plastic swivel chair and opens her laptop. The mail icon at the bottom of her screen has a little red number '1'. She excitedly clicks onto it. The unread email in her inbox is a reply from Dr Julie Owen. "Dad, she's replied already!" Seren screams down the stairs.

Her Dad can be heard bounding up the stairs two at a time and Seren is glad that her dad clearly shares her excitement. He enters Seren's room and peers over her head at the screen while Seren reads the email out loud.

~~~

Dear Seren,

I was delighted to receive your email. It is indeed very exciting that the solar storm we are experiencing means there is a high chance that the aurora can be viewed tonight from your home in South Wales.

I am indeed Welsh, as you guessed. My family is from Brecon. Have you been there? My parents still live there, but I work and live in Southampton. However, right now, I am in the Artic Circle in a place called Svalbard. I am here with some members of the Space Environment Physics group who also work at the University of Southampton. We are using a camera called ASK to take photos of the aurora. When we return to England next week, we will upload these images, and they will become part of the 'Aurora Zoo citizen science project' that you mentioned in your email.

We are here on a two-week-long science expedition, and today is the twelfth day of our observations of the northern lights. We've actually had to extend our stay here by two days because we have so much to do. I'm accompanied by Dr Dan Winter and his student Charlie Helens. They are very busy right now making sure the camera is working properly. When it is all set up, the ASK camera will take photos of the aurora at the same time as we use the big radar dish outside to take measurements.

The dish sends radio waves towards the aurora in the upper part of the Earth's atmosphere. The aurora reflects the waves back to Earth, and we collect information from them as they hit the radar dish again. While Dr Dan and Charlie are setting up I thought I would sneak away and use my free time to reply to your email.

The reason you might see the aurora in South Wales tonight is because the Sun is currently very active, it's actually in what we call it's 'Solar Maximum'. What this means is that the Sun is sending out a lot more energetic particles than it usually does. This is why we are here in Svalbard, because more activity from the Sun means it's more likely we can see the aurora from here in the Arctic Circle. If we do get lots of bright aurora then we have a lot more data to analyse, which is great. Us scientists love collecting data, especially when it means coming to a cool place like Svalbard!

Anyway, all this extra activity from the Sun means that it is sending out a lot more charged particles than usual. Sometimes the particles get pushed out very suddenly into space in what we call a Coronal Mass Ejection (CME), and that's what happened last night. When a CME happens a very large amount of these particles gets sent out from the Sun in a big burst. We know the speed the burst was ejected from the Sun, and we know that it is coming in the direction of our Earth. This large amount of energetic particles will reach the Earth tonight, around 6pm UK time, and interact with something called the Magnetosphere. This is just the name for the region around the Earth where the magnetic field is very strong. The particles from the Sun get trapped inside the Magnetosphere and then get pushed down even further into Earth's atmosphere. As you know, the upper atmosphere has lots of oxygen in it and these particles from the Sun can bump into the oxygen and cause it to glow green or red. If the particles have enough energy, they can get even further down in our atmosphere to the nitrogen gas which glows pink, but that's quite rare!

The part of Earth's atmosphere where the particles are more likely to get pushed down into is known *as the 'auroral oval'. For the Northern part of the Earth, this means the aurora will mainly happen in the air over the Arctic Circle. This is why people usually go to places like Iceland, or Lapland, and Norway, where I am right now, to see the northern lights. If you have a globe at home have a look at that, there should be a line around it called 'The Arctic Circle'.*

If you think of the Earth as a round head, the bit that gets lit up by the aurora is like a crown on top of that head. The crown of the aurora, scientifically known as 'the auroral oval' is usually quite small so you only see the aurora in the night sky above you if you are in the countries I listed above. The aurora happens in the Southern Hemisphere as well, where it is seen from Antarctica by the penguins and scientists there. The shapes the aurora makes in both the southern and northern hemispheres are symmetrical, which is really interesting to the aurora scientists. However, for the purpose of my explanation we only need to worry about what is going on in the top, northern part of the Earth.

Because the current solar storm means more and more particles are sent out from the Sun, the auroral oval – the crown on top of the head - gets stretched out. So, the position where the crown meets the Earth moves further down. Think of it like putting on a crown designed for an adult like your mam, as opposed to a small crown designed for the head size of a ten-year-old girl. The stretching of the auroral oval over the top of the Earth means that now it can be seen lower down on the Earth. Instead of it being only visible from those countries in the Arctic Circle, it has now moved south over the UK.

Even if the storm means the stretching downwards of the auroral oval happens tonight keep in mind that it is unlikely the aurora will be overhead. If it is visible from Wales, it will probably be seen low down on the horizon. You will need to look into the north of the sky. If you need help finding North use a smart phone app like 'Stellarium' or even a compass if you have one. The aurora may look quite grey to begin with but if you give your eyes enough time to adjust to the darkness and if its bright enough you should be able to see the red and green lights of the aurora. You said you live on a hill, that's perfect because you need a clear view of the horizon, with no trees or mountains in the way. Make sure you wear warm clothes as viewing the aurora can take a lot of time and requires much patience.

I do hope you get to see the aurora tonight, Seren. I have only ever seen it from here in Svalbard. I think it would be so magical to see it in my hometown with my family. I have an hour free tomorrow at 5pm UK time while the space scientists set up the ASK camera again. I would be happy to talk to you on Zoom if you want to know more about our camera and what we are doing here in the radar control room.

Happy Sky Watching,

Dr Julie Owen
Astronomy Outreach Leader

~~~

"Woah I can't believe she replied so quickly Dad!" exclaims Seren.

"I can't believe you understand all this stuff Seren. I bet Dr Owen doesn't get many emails from ten-year-olds that know as much as you," says Garry, looking at his daughter with pride.

Smiling to herself, Seren swivels on her chair, flicking her mousy curls from her face to look up at her dad. "I dunno about that dad, but I am not going to come with you and Mam tomorrow when you take Bili for his walk. I am going to talk to Dr Owen instead!" she announces.

Garry laughs, "Well, I am sure we can just take him earlier. I'd like to say hello to her myself, and besides, we wouldn't be very good parents if we left our ten-year-old in the house on her own!"

Chapter 3

Seren struggles with understanding time. She either overestimates how much time she has or severely underestimates it. Even though it was 5pm by the time she was back downstairs that evening, a full hour before the weather lady said it would be dark enough to watch the aurora, she felt like all she could do with that hour was wait.

Getting her arctic explorer gear on only took about 5 minutes so now she sits on the stairs, dressed in her favourite purple fleece, woolly yellow bobble hat, purple wellies and purple puffer coat. Seren's favourite colour is purple, obviously, but her Mam said a purple bobble hat would be too much purple. Seren remembered that her teacher said that yellow and purple were complimentary colours, so she thought the yellow bobble hat was the best compromise. Her Dad also said the yellow hat would stop her looking too much like a massive blueberry.

Seren sits on the stairs in all her layers, it's now 5.10pm and her look of sheer determination has become more a look of distress. Her mam, feeling a bit sorry for her daughter, goes into the living room to retrieve Seren's favourite fidget, a yellow and orange tangle toy. Seren previously had a purple and teal tangle toy, but she lost it in the airport while on holiday to Tenerife.

Now at 5.15pm, with 45 minutes before it gets dark, Seren sits, twirling her fidget around her left hand while frantically bouncing her right leg inside her wellington boot. Bili looks up at her with his big dark eyes, with his favourite tennis ball (which is very mangled because of all the indoor ball time with Seren's dad), dangles by a thread of fabric from his mouth.

At 5.30, Seren decides she can't wait anymore and goes out into the back garden with Bili traipsing behind her, wagging his long, fluffy tail. She grabs her purple camping chair on the way past the back gate. Garry eyes his daughter from the back window of the house. He chuckles to himself because from his view, there in the warm living room, not a single star is visible. However, determined as always, his daughter, looks up in all directions as large and ominous fluffy clouds move across the horizon.

It is not a lucky night for Seren.

By 6.05pm the sun is fully set but the sky is also full of thick clouds. Not even the group of bright stars that Seren calls 'the saucepan' are visible. Seren loves using the saucepan to find the North Star, she does it whenever it's dark and clear and then tells whoever she is with, which is usually her parents, which direction is north and which direction is south. Her parents, they support her love of astronomy, of course, but they have got really tired of her telling them this each time - where the saucepan is and how to use it. Because, after all, like her mam says, "North is always in that direction Seren, it never changes."

In her excitement to see the aurora, Seren has not actually sat down in her camping chair yet. After figuring out where north is, which she had to do with the 'SkyView Lite' app on her phone because of the lack of visible 'saucepan', Seren has been standing like a statue facing north ever since. She stays outside for a full 43 minutes seeing nothing but clouds, but she doesn't give up hope.

And even though Seren has very little patience she has remembered that Dr Owen said she needed to be patient to be a good aurora watcher, so, somehow, she has found some. She keeps her neck arched back, even though it is starting to ache, watching the clouds for any slight flicker of green or red.

"Come on in out of the cold Seren, it looks like it was a false alarm. No aurora here tonight!" says Stella, very seriously, whilst standing in the doorway.

"No Mam, I am staying here to wait, just in case. Please let me just have another 39 minutes!" Seren shouts, while not taking her eyes from the horizon.

Her mam doesn't question why Seren says 39 minutes and not 40 minutes, because she knows her daughter doesn't like even numbers, and loves the number 9. Finally, after another 22 minutes (not 39!) her mam is able to lure her back into the house with the promise of a hot chocolate, with marshmallows, of course, and a dental chew for Bili.

"I am so disappointed, Mam," Seren announces as she undoes her coat and plonks herself onto the grey leather sofa in the living room. "What am I going to talk to Dr Owen about tomorrow?" asks Seren angrily.

"Well," Stella starts, "I am sure there are lots of questions you can ask her about the work she and the space scientists are doing in Svalbard. Maybe she can tell you the name of an aurora app we can download so we get a notification the next time the aurora will be visible from Wales!"

Seren truly hopes that there is a next time.

Chapter 4

Seren's first day back in school for the new term does not go as quickly as she would have liked. Seren loves school, but some of the people in her class call her as a 'swot', 'a geek' and 'a know it all'. Seren used to get upset being called names, but after much discussion with her mam she now replies to the name calling with, "I just love to learn, so if that makes me a geek then I am proud to be one." Because she is no longer upset by the name calling, she gets called these names a lot less. Some people still think she is weird or different, but thankfully Seren has learned to embrace her weirdness and not see it as a bad thing. It would be a very boring world indeed, if everyone was the same.

Seren goes to one of the larger primary schools in the South Wales valleys, Oakwood Junior school. The school is a one-storey, red brick building with two big playgrounds: one with tarmac and one with grass. Seren prefers to play on grass, but they're only allowed onto the grass field on special occasions like sports day. Last summer, Seren won the egg and spoon race and the relay for the red team. She would have won the hurdles too if it wasn't for a magpie that distracted her near the finish line.

On average, it takes Seren 7 minutes 20 seconds to walk to school, and 9 minutes 10 seconds to walk back; she's timed it on her Fitbit and calculated the average time over the last 420 days. Technically children in the UK don't learn to do averages until year 6 but Seren has already taught herself. The walk home takes longer because it is up hill; it's the valleys, there are hills everywhere.

Seren's best friend is called India, and it's India's dad who walks them both to school. India and Seren live in the same street, if Seren runs as fast as she can she can get to India's house from her own door step in under one minute! India's dad doesn't need to be at work by 9am like Seren's parents because he is an illustrator. India says that means he is a 'Freelancer' and can work however much he likes.

Both India and Seren were born in September which makes them two of the oldest children in year 5. India is 9 days younger than Seren and they have been friends since they were only one years old, when their mams took them both to the same mother and baby group.

There are three year 5 classes at Oakwood Juniors. Each class has a different name themed around the 'Three Peak Challenge', the three highest mountains in the UK. Their headmistress came up with this naming convention because she is obsessed with the challenge and has completed it 7 times.

Seren and India are in the same class. Their class was called 'Snowdon' after the highest peak in Wales, but ever since the Snowdownia National Park Authority changed the mountain's name to 'Yr Wyddfa' the class have been going through a bit of an identity crisis. There are 33 children in the Yr Wyddfa class, and their teacher is called Mrs Davies.

Mrs Davies wears tight clothes, like jeggings and tight-fitted dresses. Whatever she wears it's always black. One of the students once asked her if she dressed like that because she was actually a ninja. Mrs Davies simply replied, "I'm not a ninja no, just a teacher, but if I was a ninja I probably wouldn't be able to tell you!" So, it's still a bit of a mystery as to whether Mrs Davies is in fact a part-time ninja.

Mrs Davies has dark brown straight hair, that dangles just past her shoulders and is parted in the middle. Seren thinks Mrs Davies has a kind face. Seren doesn't really know what it means, to have a kind face, but it was what her mam said when she met Mrs Davies during a parents evening once. She is a kind teacher though, so I guess that means Seren's mam is right, and her face matches her personality. Her mam is usually right about things, not that Seren will admit that to her.

That morning, the first day back after Christmas holidays, 'Tuesday 2nd January', Seren knows the date because she just wrote it into the top of her workbook on a fresh page and carefully underlined it with her yellow ruler and favourite pen, which is of course purple, but has black ink, purple ink isn't allowed sadly.

Seren is sat at the table right at the front of class. On Seren's table is India, Ally, Caleb, Aled, Dani, and Grace and their teaching assistant Miss Jones. Seren is even more restless and distracted than normal; she taps her left leg ferociously up and down and spins her pencil in her right hand like she's leading a jazz band. Her mind wanders out the window.

Mrs Davies stands at the smart board at the front of the class. She's struggling to get the children excited about a 'Negative Numbers' math sheet. Seren turns away from the window to look over at India, who is busy working through the worksheet; she is already on number 7, and Seren hasn't even started yet.

It's like there's a weight in Seren's mind, making everything harder and heavier than normal, and she can't get started, she can't lift her pen, it all seems so too much, just doing tasks she normally finds easy. So, Seren just goes back to her window gazing.

When Seren is waiting for something important to happen, like her meeting with Dr Owen later, she finds it hard to focus on anything else; it's like her brain is already too full of excitement and expectation. All she can do is wait, wasting the time in anticipation for the thing that will happen soon. However, Seren starts to feel guilty about not finishing her worksheet like Mrs Davies asked. She also feels increasingly moody at the idea that India will get a better mark than her on the worksheet, even though India isn't as good at maths as Seren.

While Seren continues to gaze out the window in what she calls her 'waiting mode', she decides that she's feeling even more moody than that time her family drove all the way to the science museum in Cardiff, over 45 minutes away, only to find it closed. That day, even a raspberry ripple ice cream on the waterfront couldn't calm her.

Mrs Davies, sensing that she's losing the children to the tedium of 'Negative Numbers', claps her hands together twice. All the children clap their hands twice in response and look to her with anticipation written across their young faces. Mrs Davies turns to the children with excitement and says, "Yr Wyddfas, please put down your pens. I have an announcement to make. As you know, we have just started a new term, and that means we can start to learn some new subjects. This term we are going to be studying all about Space! We will be learning all about the Sun, Moon and the planets of the Solar System. What do you think about that?"

Seren finally turns away from the window at this unexpected announcement from Mrs Davies. Afterall it's polite to look at someone when they are speaking to you, even if you don't look at their eyes, and just look at that space on the top of their head between their eyebrows. But she's nowhere near as excited as the rest of the class, and as they jump about with happiness, Seren sits thinking about her call later, with just the heavy weight of her 'waiting mode'.

Chapter 5

As hungry children queue noisy around Seren she clutches at her galaxy-themed lunch, she is still lost in her own thoughts, even while all around her is utter chaos. India is waiting patiently for her to open her lunch box to see if she has any food worth swapping.

Seren did manage to hyper-focus and finish her maths worksheet before the lunch bell rang but she is still all moody and distracted. Not even the discovery of a massive bit of leftover chocolate log in her lunch box, when she finally opens it, does the job of cheering her up. India is sat opposite her at the long lunch table with her matching lunch box (a lot of India and Seren's stuff is both matching and space themed) and she gazes at her best friend through her short black afro curls.

"Seren, what is wrong with you today?" asks India, "You've been talking about doing the Space curriculum in year 5 since we started in Reception class, and now that we are about to actually start it, you don't seem to be excited at all!" India pauses, her face full of confusion because of Seren's lack of excitement. "Even Ben Evans seemed excited about us finally studying Space, did you see him swinging his arms about? He almost hit Ally in the nose. You know Ben Evans is normally only interested in being naughty or annoying Mrs Davies," says India, looking very seriously at her moody best friend.

"I am excited, India!" replies Seren, looking at India with her best effort at an excited face, "I am just really annoyed I didn't get to see the aurora last night. I am talking to an Astrophysicist tonight at 5 o'clock on Zoom. She's in Norway right now and I just feel like I can't focus because I am waiting for that to happen. I just can't get excited about anything else right now, and besides, I think Dr Owen will know more about Space than Mrs Davies!"

"Why are you speaking so fast? You normally speak fast, but that was even faster than normal. And what is the Aurora? Who is Dr Owen?" asks India, looking incredibly confused while finally taking a bite from her red sauce sandwich.

After school has finished, Seren and India walk home together with India's dad lagging behind them. It only takes 8 minutes and 55 seconds to get to India's, 15 seconds faster than Seren's average; she really wants to get back for the video call with Dr Owen! Even though it's only 3:43pm and the call isn't until 5pm, all Seren can do is wait. Seren normally goes over to India's house to do homework after school, but today she just runs straight home.

Seren goes straight up to her room and plonks herself down with purpose in her purple swivel chair. Poor Bili has been trying to get her attention ever since she came through the door. He was all excited because she was home early. He's trying all his tricks: looking at her with his 'puppy dog eyes', rolling on his back with his legs in the air, and his belly on display, and holding his fluffy tomato toy in his mouth and looking all cute.

Once comfy in her swivel chair, Seren finally gives Bili some attention. Looking down into his big brown eyes, Seren places her hand onto Bili's head; she can feel his excitement and unconditional love, but that's always there. Nothing else comes through. They regularly have their 'mind conversations' when she gets home from school; Bili mainly wants to know more about the school dog, a cavapoo called Winston. Seren doesn't know if Bili can count, but he always seems to want to know how many belly rubs Winston has received from her, it's like he's a bit jealous and wants to make sure he always gets more.

Only Seren's dad and India know about her ability to 'hear' the thoughts of dogs. Seren has not been able to thoroughly test whether her ability works with other animals. One time she tried it on a goat at the petting zoo, because she had been petting his head for quite a while, but she couldn't sense anything. Seren wondered if the child near her, that was tempting the goat with a large leaf, had distracted it. Apparently, goats will eat literally anything, and Seren can very much relate to being distracted by food. Seren's dad says that to know for certain, she would need to test it with another animal that feels comfortable in her presence and is ok with her touching its head for a few minutes. The only other animal that might be comfortable with Seren is their goldfish, they have had him for almost two years and he's called Moron, which is Welsh for carrot, and carrots are also orange. But she's not sure how she would go about putting her hand on Moron's head while he is swimming about in his tank, especially because his head is probably only the size of Seren's little finger.

Sometimes, like today, Bili doesn't seem to have any clear thoughts coming through. Seren is just about to give up and move her hand from his fluffy head and open her laptop when she senses that Bili does have a question.

"Seren, when you talk to the scientist later can you ask her if she likes dogs?"

Chapter 6

By 4.45pm has Seren finished her tea, which was fish fingers, beans, and chips with red sauce. She insisted on eating it at her desk, in front of her laptop with Zoom open, just in case Dr Owen decided to call her early. Seren's Dad sits on her yellow armchair, eagerly looking over her shoulder. Her mam is downstairs feeding Bili. While waiting for this long-awaited call, Seren writes down some questions she wants to ask Dr Owen:

- What did you have for your tea?
- How cold is it in Svalbard today?
- What are the other scientists doing while you are Zooming me?
- When can I next see the aurora from South Wales?
- Have you ever seen the pink aurora?
- Is there such thing as purple aurora?
- Is there aurora happening outside there right now?
- Do you like dogs?

Just as Seren is about to add a question about polar bears, her laptop starts ringing and a window pops up at the centre of the screen saying, 'Julie Owen calling'. "Oh my god Dad! Dr Owen is calling, quick quick!" exclaims Seren, scrambling for the mouse.

Dr Julie Owen's face fills the screen, and Seren is a bit disappointed that she's not wearing the same purple puffer coat she saw her wearing in the team photograph on the Aurora Zoo webpage. Dr Owen is wearing a grey fleece. Her hair is blonde and curly, just like Seren's, and she has nice teeth, something Seren can only notice because Julie is smiling. It's a kind smile.

"Hello Seren, I am so glad to meet you. Is that your dad in the background?" says Dr Owen.

"Yes, that's my dad, he's called Garry and he's sitting in my yellow chair, which is his favourite chair to nap in, but don't worry about him. I've been waiting to chat to you all day, Dr Owen. I have so many questions!" replies Seren excitedly.

"That's great, and please call me Julie. I'm happy to answer all your questions, but before I do, I thought I could show you around the control room and introduce you to the space scientists who are here with me. They are about to start using the radar and camera to collect data and images of the aurora for their research. They said that before they start, they would be happy to chat to you. I am using my phone so I'll just spin the camera around so you can see everything I can see," says Dr Owen.

"That sounds great!" replies Seren.

As Dr Owen moves closer to the many screens that cover the walls at head height, Seren sees two people in desk chairs below them who look like they are typing. One of them has straight, white-blonde hair, and the other has short brown hair, both wearing matching grey fleeces. Seren thinks this must be a space scientist uniform or something.

"Dr Dan, Charlie, I want to introduce you to Seren," says Dr Owen.

Dr Owen passes her phone to Dr Dan, the one with the short dark hair, and he switches the screen around so that Seren and him are face-to-face. "Hey, Seren, my name is Dr Dan Winter, I have been to Svalbard about 17 times, and I designed and built the camera we use to take images of the aurora, which is called the ASK camera. ASK stands for Aurora Structure and Kinetics. The camera is called this because we are interested in the 'Structure' of the aurora which means the shapes it makes in the sky. 'Kinetics' means movement, so we also want to see how it moves. Does that make sense?" says Dr Dan looking into the phone.

"Oh yes, that makes lots of sense. That's so cool that you built it yourself Dr Dan. I could never do anything like that!"

'I am sure you could Seren. It just takes lots of studying. I've always liked taking things apart and trying to put them back together, ever since I was a young child, so it makes sense that I ended up in this job. I'll pass you over to my PhD student Charlie now,' says Dr Dan, passing the phone over.

"Hi Seren, my name is Charlie Helens. I am in the second year of my PhD studies working under Dan's supervision. I am hoping to finish my aurora research in another two years and then I will be a doctor too, which is pretty cool. Tonight is the first time Dan has put me in charge of setting up the observations on the radar, so I need to make sure I double-check everything. I don't want to mess that up. Shall I tell you more about the radar and the camera?" asks Charlie.

"Yes, definitely," replies Seren. Charlie smiles back because he loves talking about his work. "Well, the radar will be looking into the same area of sky that the ASK camera is taking images of. The information from the radar will eventually tell us things like what the temperature of the atmosphere is where the aurora is happening. The scientists who research weather patterns on Earth use this information to determine the upper atmosphere's temperature."

Seren interrupts Charlie, speaking faster than her normal speed, "Oh, a scientist who researches the weather is called a meteorologist, right? I learned that from a book I read just before Christmas. I got obsessed with learning about different shapes of cloud. My favourite cloud type is a 'cumulus' because those are the ones you see from the plane if you go on holiday, and they look like you could go to sleep in them all cwtched up" replies Seren excitedly.

"Cwtch! I love that word; does it really mean cuddle in Welsh? I thought Dr Owen made it up," Charlie laughs, "and yes, Seren, that's right, they are called meteorologists, although the ones who use this radar, we normally call them climate scientists," Charlie says still smiling. "Did you want to know anything more about the radar or the camera that we will be using tonight?"

"Oh yes, I definitely do," says Seren, a little flustered, looking down at her list of questions. "I am so sorry Charlie, I got so excited I went off subject and started talking about clouds, it happens all the time when I get excited, I just blurt out facts, my mam says I need to be careful because some people might think I am being rude, especially when I interrupt them. I don't mean to be rude." Seren looks back down at her notebook, "Urgh, I don't have any questions written down for you. I thought I would only get to speak to Dr Owen tonight, so I only prepared questions for her," Seren scrunches up her face in frustration, while Charlie looks on quizzically. Thankfully, a question comes to her: "Oh I just thought of one, what is a radar? I thought it was something they used in the war?"

"Yes, that's right. Radar can be used in war times to determine if enemy aircraft are nearby. It works by sending out radio waves and then seeing if anything, like an aeroplane, gets in the way and reflects those waves back toward the dish. If you get a reflected radio wave then that means there is something in the wave's path. A radar is just a dish with a receiver in the centre, same as you might have seen on the side of people's houses to get 'Sky TV', but the one we use here in Svalbard is much bigger. The Sky TV dishes can only receive the radio waves from the satellites in space, our radar are different because they can send and receive. We send radio waves high up into the atmosphere, and if there is aurora happening, the radio waves are reflected back down into the dish. We can tell from the energy of the waves we receive in the dish what kind of aurora did the reflecting. Does that make sense, Seren?"

"I think so, Charlie. Thank you for explaining it" says Seren. She tries hard, but she can't resist telling him some extra facts she's just thought of. "Now I think about it, I have seen a documentary about some scientists who were looking for the Loch Ness monster in Scotland, and they were using radar, I think, but with the radio waves bouncing off the bottom of the big lake?"

"Ahhh, I think what you are describing is something called sonar, not radar, but the idea is the same. The main difference is that we are using radio waves in radar, and they travel at the speed of light. For sonar they use ultrasonic waves that travel at the speed of sound," answers Charlie, he's smiling because he is very impressed with Seren's knowledge and enthusiasm for science. "By the way, did the scientists in the documentary find anything in the Loch?" he asks.

Before Seren can answer Charlie, she notices a big husky dog sleeping under the desk behind him. "Oh my, is that your dog? Do you get to take your dog to work?"

"Oh, that's Milo," says Charlie turning in his desk chair to look back at the mound of black, white and grey fur. "I wish he was my dog, but Milo is the engineer's dog. The engineer is called Austen. He lives here in the settlement we are in right now, which is called Longyearbyen. Austen has to be in the control room when we are using the radar as he is the expert, and he can fix stuff if it breaks. A lot of people in Svalbard have huskies that they use to pull their sleds, but Milo is actually so old he doesn't do much sled pulling these days. He does lots of sleeping under the desk though,' chuckles Charlie.

"Well, it's been lovely chatting with you, Seren, but Dr Dan and I are going to have to get going with our observations. Because we are above the Arctic Circle here in Longyearbyen, we don't have to wait until 6 o'clock for it to get dark because it's dark twenty-four hours a day right now. I'll hand Dr Owen her phone back so she can continue chatting to you. Bye." says Charlie as he disappears off the screen.

Dr Owen's face reappears and Seren is momentarily distracted by her dad snoring loudly behind her.

"Hi again, Seren, I will take the rest of this conversation in another room so as not to disturb Dr Dan and Charlie when they are setting up the radar."

All Seren can see on the screen is the carpet, so as she waits for Dr Owen to come back into view, she looks down at her list of questions. Seren tries to make her brain focus, and for the rest of the call she makes a serious goal for herself. She will only as Dr Owen the questions she has written down, and she will ask them in order. It's going to be a challenge, but she will try not to get distracted by asking her all the many questions that are now filling her mind after talking to Charlie and Dr Dan. Everything she has learned so far about being a space scientist in Svalbard is so interesting and wonderful.

And like her Nan always says, "It's important to question things Seren."

Her Nan is right, but still, she needs to focus on just the questions she has written down.

Chapter 7

When Dr Owen's face reappears on the screen, Seren is ready. She blurts out, "Dr Owen, what did you have for your tea? I had fish fingers, beans and chips and red sauce!" Julie starts to laugh at this unexpected line of questioning, and then states seriously, "I haven't had tea yet Seren. Because it's dark all the time here, we've been getting up and going to sleep at very strange times. Last night we were up using the radar until 5am in the morning. I only actually had my breakfast an hour ago."

"Oh, OK," says Seren looking back down at her list, "so how cold is it in Svalbard today?"

"Well, it has been about minus 23 degrees Celsius! Seren, it is so cold that the hairs inside your nose and eyelashes start to freeze if you are outside too long. But don't worry, we wear lots of layers, and I have a big scarf I wrap around my whole face. I really feel the cold myself so if I go outside I have 3 sets of wool base layers on, 3 coats with my big purple one on the outside, and 2 pairs of wool socks."

Seren responds to Dr Owen, "I really like your purple coat. I said that to my dad when we first saw the photo of you online, is purple your favourite colour too?"

Dr Owen is about to respond when there is a big bang from behind her. Someone wearing a balaclava, like the ones people wear to rob a bank, come through the office door. Seren's first thought is that this is probably just normal Svalbard head gear, given what Dr Owen just said about your nose hairs freezing, but the side of Dr Owen's face that is still visible looks very scared right now. Seren starts to suspect this isn't actually normal Svalbard head wear and that Dr Owen doesn't know these people.

The person wearing the balaclava shouts in a deep voice and a thick accent, "Hang up the call now!"

Only one of Dr Owen's eyes is visible on the screen but it's enough to make it clear to Seren that she is terrified. A black-gloved hand comes toward the screen and the call ends.

"Oh my gosh! Dad!" Seren spins around in her chair with her phone clutched tightly in her hand. "Dad!" she screams, "Wake up! This is important!" She shakes the arm of the yellow armchair frantically.

Garry stirs from his sleep and sits up all confused. He can see from his daughter's face that she is very distressed. "Oh gosh, Seren. Sorry I fell asleep, that yellow chair really is rather cwtchy. What's wrong? You look upset?"

"Dad, I think Dr Owen has been kidnapped by some bank robbers. They made her end the call, and they had a funny accent." Seren declares, as she stands up from her swivel chair looking very seriously at her dad.

"No, I am sure that can't be right? Why do you think they are bank robbers?" he says, looking confused.

"They had those things on that cover your whole face, with little holes in for eyes. I think you call them, bal-ac-lavas?" she says all flustered, trying to remember the proper word. "And before you say, 'they are just wearing them because it's cold'; this all happened inside!"

"But you said they are bank robbers? Dr Owen isn't in a bank Seren, what are you on about? Maybe they were other scientists who had just arrived at the radar station and had forgotten to take their balaclavas off when they came inside. I think she probably wasn't expecting them to appear, and she accidentally hung up. Let's see if she calls you back. I am sure she will."

"No, Dad, you didn't see her face, she was so scared. They shouted at her to 'hang up now!' Surely other scientists wouldn't be so rude!" announces Seren. Garry looks at his daughter with concern and rises from the chair to give her a cwtch.

"I am sure Dr Owen is ok," he says. "Let's go downstairs and have a nice cup of tea, I'll let you have one of the Foxes chocolate rounds you like; I know where your mother keeps her secret stash. Bring your phone down with you just in case she calls back."

Seren follows her dad and Bili down the stairs. She has a bad feeling in her tummy. She knows something isn't right, but when an adult tells you that you have misunderstood something and you have only been on the planet for 10 years and they have been here 27 years more than you, then you start to doubt yourself. Adults know almost everything. Don't they? Although Seren's Dad was asleep through the whole thing, so how can he really know for sure?

By the time it gets to 7:30pm, which is Seren's official bedtime (even though she is rarely in bed much before 8.30pm), Dr Owen has not called back. Seren called her back on Zoom at 6.45pm and then got her dad to try at 6.47pm. Seren also emailed Dr Owen twice to ask if she was ok but there was no reply.

Tonight, it is Seren's mam's turn to do the bedtime story so she leads Seren up the stairs, trailed by Bili, of course. Stella tries to reassure her daughter, and as they all enter Seren's room her mam says, "I know you are worried about Dr Owen, but I am sure there is a perfectly reasonable explanation. Please try not to worry. Maybe they just don't have good internet there, and it just cut out. That would explain why she hasn't called you back or replied."

Seren looks up at her mam unconvinced. "Of course they have good internet Mam, you are being silly. They are doing important aurora research where they need the internet to work all the time, and besides she was replying to my emails very quickly yesterday."

Chapter 8

Seren has a bad day in school the next day. She tries her very best to listen to her parent's advice and not to worry about Dr Owen. She wants to believe that everything is fine and there's a simple explanation. But she can't stop thinking back to the anger in the man's voice telling Dr Owen to hang up the call.

Mrs Davies is used to Seren being distracted in class and is usually very patient with her, but today even Mrs Davies can't figure out how to help her. Seren is the only student in Yr Wyddfa class today who doesn't finish her English worksheet.

By the time Seren is 4 minutes 35 seconds into her walk home from school with India and India's dad she already has a fully thought-out plan to save Dr Owen. India's dad is talking about a children's book he is illustrating with a magical baby elephant and doesn't even notice that Seren isn't listening to a word he is saying. If Seren's parents won't help her, then she will have to find some people who will.

Her plan is to get on the train to Southampton, and go to the University, and find the other scientists from the Space Environment Physics group and tell them what has happened. She's been on the train to Southampton before, when her nan took her on a day out to Bournemouth beach. Seren never actually saw any of Southampton itself, just the train station when they changed onto the train that went to Bournemouth, but she doesn't think it can be that hard to get to the University from the train station. She can check on Google maps when she gets home.

Seren's mam tries to engage her in conversation as soon as she steps through the door, Stella always like to ask Seren about her day, and Seren is usually very happy to tell her, in graphic detail, about what she has learned. But today Seren runs straight past her mam, head down, focused, scaling the stairs two at a time. She slams her bedroom door behind her. Bili doesn't get chance to give his usual greeting either and he gazes longingly up the stairs at Seren's door, holding his tomato toy in his mouth.

After some quick Googling Seren thinks her best option will be to get the number 56 bus to Newport tomorrow morning at 9.35am (which stops just outside her school; she has seen the college students catching it). She will have to think up an excuse to stay outside the school gates so that India goes in without her. When the bus arrives in Newport it stops right outside the train station. She will then need to buy a train ticket to Southampton Central and then get the U1C or U1B bus to the University of Southampton. It seems simple enough. Hopefully, if she can make the 10.44 train from Newport, she will arrive at Southampton by 13.05.

Seren estimates she will need to get £70 out of her piggy bank for the buses and the return train ticket. Although, what she will do when she gets back to Wales after she has told the other space scientists what has happened is not on her mind. All she can focus on is telling them that the rest of their team is in danger in Svalbard, and they need to get help to them as soon as possible.

~

Outside the school gates the next day India stands
with Seren, she is wondering why Seren has
suddenly stopped moving and why they aren't
walking into school. India hates being late and
Seren is always late. "Seren you are awfully quiet
again this morning, is there another aurora going off
tonight or something?" asks India, looking with
concern at her best friend who is still not moving
towards the open gate.

"No aurora tonight, no. I am just worrying about
that worksheet I didn't finish yesterday, I am so
annoyed at myself for not being able to finish it off. I
really hate my brain sometimes!" Seren replies. She
doesn't even need to lie. Her brain really does annoy
her when it gets too full, especially when it means
she is behind on her schoolwork.

After waving goodbye to India's Dad and making
sure he is out of sight around the corner, Seren
decides to put her plan into action. "Oh no, India!"
she cries, looking down at her wrist, "I've lost my
gold bracelet that I got from my nan for my tenth

birthday, I need to walk back and check if it's dropped off on the floor."

"But Seren, the bell is about to go for the start of school," responds India, hurriedly. She bends down and starts looking around the pavement to help her friend, but she is clearly very distressed at the thought of being late.

"Don't worry India. I can run back up the road really fast and catch up to your dad. I'll ask him to check the rest of the way home for it. I'll be right back. Don't worry, just go on in!" India looks at her friend with some suspicion as she is shooed away, but she really does hate being late, so she turns and runs into the school playground just as the bell rings out for the start of school.

Seren waits till there are no adults or children in sight then goes quickly to the bus stop. She is the only one there and as she waits. She stares down intently at the hands on her watch; Seren actually wears two watches, one on each wrist. Her Fitbit on her left wrist and her analogue watch on the right.

She watches the second hand move on her analogue watch. It has a pink nebula on the face and the minute and hour hands of the watch are astronaut arms and hands. The astronaut, in the middle, has blonde hair just like hers. Some people think it's weird that she wears two watches, but she thinks it makes perfect sense, surely two is better than one.

The bus arrives three minutes late, but Seren didn't notice it was late because she was daydreaming about being an astronaut surrounded by pink nebula while doing an EVA.

Seren chooses a seat toward the back of the bus, on the right-hand side, as far away from other people as she can be. She is surprised the bus driver did not quiz her on why she, a ten-year-old, was catching a bus alone, but luckily the driver seems to be having a 'bit of a moment'. He asked the old lady who got on after Seren if he could see her student bus pass, to which the old lady responded, "You flatter me young man, but I am sixty-eight years old! Although, I guess I am a student of life."

Chapter 9

At the train station in Newport, Seren uses the machines to buy her ticket because she wants to avoid speaking to any people who might be likely to question her being there. She times going through the ticket barrier with a young mother pushing her baby in a pram. She hopes that anyone passing by would assume that Seren is with them. Luckily, the mother and baby also head towards platform 4 for the Southampton train and Seren makes sure to sit near them to continue disguising the fact she is on her own. As morning rush hour is over the train is very quiet and Seren makes it all the way to Southampton without anyone questioning her.

When Seren exits the train station, she notices that the weather is much better here in Southampton than it is in Wales. She needs to find the nearest bus stop so she takes out her phone and opens up the Map app. The app says she can take the 13:22 U2B bus from the bus stop and it will arrive at the University campus at 13.45, which is perfect. Seren puts her over-ear purple headphones on to try and deter anyone at the bus stop from talking to her. There is an old lady with a tartan pull-along shopping basket who is looking at suspiciously at her, so Seren quickly turns around so that she is facing away from the old lady, towards a man wearing blue overalls covered in paint, he's not looking at her, he's looking down at his phone. She faces toward him because she guesses he is much less likely to question her than the old lady, whatever he is looking at on his phone is clearly very fascinating to him.

Finally, a bright blue double decker bus pulls up at the bus stop, Seren slides down her headphones onto her neck and steps onto the bus. She mumbles, "a return to the University please," and presents the driver with a £10 note. He looks back at her sternly and then waves his hand toward the back of the bus "Kid, I don't have any change. Just get on." Seren doesn't like the fact the driver seems annoyed at her, and she also doesn't like the idea of not paying, but at least he doesn't question why she is on his bus and not in school. Seren gets a window seat toward the back of the bus and enjoys looking out the window at this new city. She tries to work out in which direction the sea is. Seren assumed, based on the map, that the sea would be easily visible from Southampton, but apparently not.

Luckily for Seren, as she gets off the bus at the University bus interchange there is a big map of the whole University campus right in front of her. All the buildings are numbered but there doesn't seem to be any order to their numbering, this makes her quite annoyed and stressed. "Why have numbered buildings if they are all in a random order. Why is building number 100 next to number 2? This is stupid," she whispers to herself, trying not to panic. Finally, in the bottom left edge of the map she sees 'Building 46', which she knows from her Googling earlier is the 'Physics and Astronomy' building. She takes a photo of the map on her phone and quickly starts walking in that direction.

The first things Seren notices is how green the campus is, and she gets quite excited when the path she's walking on goes over a little stream with some ducks paddling along and quacking away at each other.

"Hello duckies!" Seren exclaims as she walks over the bridge, and then she instantly feels silly and childish. University students pass by her, walking in the opposite direction. The students laugh at something, and Seren feels her face going bright red. She assumes they are laughing at her for greeting the ducks.

Seren can feel herself getting all stressed and embarrassed so she stops on the path to drink some water, like her mam always says, "it's good to stay hydrated." Seren hopes drinking the cold water will help reduce all the heat building up in her face, she's all red and flushed.

As she turns around to sling her water bottle back into her bag Seren notices a sign saying 'Building 46' with an up-arrow next to it. She looks into the distance at a large grey building just up the hill in front of her, that must be it. Seren walks up the hill and into the large foyer of the Physics and

Astronomy building. It dawns on her that she no idea where the space scientists' office is. She starts to panic again but then sees a big floor layout sign on the wall ahead of her, it seems that the building has 5 floors and that she is on floor 2. Seren starts to wonder where floor 1 is, how is she already on floor 2? No time to worry about that, she needs to focus.

There are students everywhere. Some rush past her, but most just stand about as if waiting for something, none of them are speaking to each other, all of them are just looking down at their phones like zombies. Seren looks at them seriously, trying to work out if any of them look like they might know the building layout. Then, weaving his way around the zombie-like students, is an older man with white hair and a rainbow lanyard with a 'Staff ID' card on, around his neck. Seren likes rainbows, rainbows make her smile, so she decides this rainbow-lanyard man might be a good person to ask for directions.

"Hello, I wonder if you can help me?" asks Seren shyly, "I am looking for the offices of the space scientists? They are these physicists who study the aurora. Do you know where their office is?"

"You are in luck," says rainbow-lanyard man, smiling down at Seren. "I do know them; I once did an outreach event with Dr Dan. They are up on the fourth floor in room 409, it's just up two more flights of stairs and then right along the corridor."

"OK, thanks Mr!" shouts Seren rushing off toward the stairs before the man can question what she is doing there.

The corridor on the fourth floor is very long, but Seren keeps on going, past lots of doors with 'LASER ON' signs, until she gets to room 409. The door has a metal plaque on it that says, 'Space Environment Physics Group', so she knows she is in the right place. Seren takes a big breath in and knocks twice. "Come in," says a muffled voice through the door.

As Seren walks into the office, she sees two women huddled around a large circular table covered with scientific papers, one of them looks about 20 years old and the other one is more like 50.

"Hello, can we help you?" says the older one. Dr Sandi Shaw and her PhD student Juliet Samuels were definitely not expecting a ten-year-old to interrupt their meeting today. "I hope so," says Seren slowly walking towards the table looking flustered. Dr Shaw is pretty good at reading people's expressions, and she can tell that Seren is indeed one very stressed young girl. She pulls out a chair next to them for Seren to sit down in.

Seren quickly blurts out the story of how she was having a Zoom call with Dr Owen in Svalbard and that people with balaclavas on told her to get off the call. Seren talks very fast as she explains how her parents wouldn't listen to her and why her only option was to come to Southampton on her own. She finishes her explanation, "so, I pretended to go to school, but I didn't, and I got on a bus and a train and another bus and now I am here. So can you help?" she pants.

"Wow. OK, that is concerning indeed." says Dr Shaw. "Before I try contact Dr Owen in Svalbard can you tell me your name? I will have to call your parents. I am sure they are very worried about you."

"Oh, yes. Sorry, my name is Seren Jones. Don't worry about my parents though. They won't even know I am gone as it's not home time yet, so India won't have told her dad I wasn't in school," replies Seren as she gets her phone out of her pocket.

Seren shows Dr Shaw her mother's number. Dr Shaw writes it down before going into her office and closing the door. Seren can see her through the internal window looking concerned. Her mam is not going to be happy with her, that's for sure!

Juliet looks up at Seren from her laptop, brushing her long dark hair behind her ear and says, "I am just checking my emails Seren, and it is a bit weird actually. Dr Dan has been emailing us every time they finish observing with the radars and camera, and we didn't receive an email from them yesterday or the day before that. I didn't notice that they hadn't emailed because me and Dr Shaw have been busy trying to finish writing my first paper."

Dr Shaw comes back into the main office, "Well you were right Seren, your mother had no idea you hadn't gone to school today. She is very worried, and it took quite a lot of convincing to get her to believe you are sitting in my office here at the University of Southampton and not at your school in South Wales. Your dad is going to drive down and pick you up now. He should hopefully be here within three hours."

Seren's first thought is that she has wasted her pocket money on that return train ticket, she starts to wonder how many creme eggs she could have bought with that money (bizarrely Easter eggs are already in the shops, despite it only being January). After thinking for a while about how lovely a creme egg would be right now, she then remembers why she came all this way. "Ok! We need to focus!" Seren exclaims. "We should use the time before my dad gets here to try figure out what happened to Dr Owen, and Dr Dan and Charlie!"

Juliet explains to Dr Shaw about the team in Svalbard and how they haven't emailed a progress report in the last two days. In response, Dr Shaw pulls out her phone and says she will go into her office and call some of their contacts at the University of Svalbard who also work at the radar and know Dr Dan. While she is in her office, Juliet brings up the Svalbard government news site. "Let's check this website; there is usually info on here about local incidents. Sometimes polar bears come into Longyearbyen, where all the people and scientists live, and they have to lockdown the area. They always post about that on this news site because the Svalbard government have their own helicopter which they use to try scare the polar bears away. Dr Dan once got trapped at the radar control room for a whole day because there was a polar bear in the valley. The polar bears used to come into Longyearbyen all the time. The husky dogs that pull the sleds are kept outside you see so the polar bear can smell their food." She pauses. "I am sure you already know Seren, but because of climate change the polar bears homes are literally melting and there's much less food for them in the sea and on the ice, so the huskie's food is very tempting when the polar bears are starving. People thought that would force them to come into town to look for food more often. And in previous years that seemed to be exactly what was happening. However, and rather strangely, we haven't had one of these polar bear incidents in Longyearbyen for over a year now," says Juliet.

The mention of husky dogs reminds Seren of Milo and how he was sound asleep under the desk when she was on the call with Dr Owen. Surely, he would have woken up when the bad man came into the control room. Milo might have seen what happened. He might still be there! If the scientists were all kidnapped, he might be there all on his own. Seren can't get her words out, her thoughts putting her all into a fluster. Eventually, she manages to get out the word "Milo."

"Oh my, you are right," says Juliet wide eyed. "Austen and Milo are always at the radar. But don't worry, I am sure that Dr Shaw will get one of our contacts to go up to the radar right now. We can make sure that whoever it is checks thoroughly to see if Milo is still there. Hopefully everyone is fine, and there's a perfectly simple explanation for all this." Seren hopes all the adults are right about this 'simple explanation', but she has a bad feeling.

She has a very bad feeling indeed.

Chapter 10

When Dr Shaw comes back into the main office after making lots of calls she informs Seren and Juliet that the space scientists, and Austen the engineer, they are all indeed missing.

"The climate scientists who are currently at the radar have checked everywhere, there is no sign of them," says Dr Shaw as she sits down at the round table next to them. "Luckily the University of Svalbard climate and space scientists all know each other. The climate scientists also use the radar for their work researching Svalbard's atmosphere and climate change. Even though we all use the radars at different times everyone knows Austen and Milo, because they are always up there." She sighs, she is clearly quite upset by what she is about to tell them. "They did find Milo." She pauses, "He was crouched under the desk in the corner of the control room shaking. It looks like he is quite badly injured, and of course he has been there on his own for two days, so they have called a vet."

"Oh no that's terrible," says Seren looking down into her hands.

"The climate scientists said they will call the Governor's office and the local police. I am sure they will do everything they can to work out what has happened." Dr Shaw pauses thoughtfully.

"I think Juliet and I will fly out to Svalbard as soon as we can to join the search. It's just a shame that dogs cannot talk, it seems that Milo is the only witness to what happened."

Seren is, of course, itching to tell Dr Shaw about her ability to communicate with dogs at this point. She doesn't say anything though, because she thinks that as a scientist Dr Shaw is going to be very sceptical of her abilities. She will surely think Seren is just a ten-year-old with an over-active imagination, which she is, but she's not imagining her abilities, they are real. If she can communicate with Bili, then she should be able to communicate with Milo; it has to work! But how can she convince

Dr Shaw to let her go all the way to Svalbard with them to talk to a husky dog?

Seren decides to wait until her dad arrives in Southampton so he can help her explain. Garry knows about her abilities after all. Maybe if he, a responsible adult, explains it, Dr Shaw will believe them. As Seren is pondering this dilemma, she looks over at Juliet's laptop where she is frantically looking up all the possible flight times from Southampton airport to Svalbard airport. It's very clear she wants to get there as soon as possible to help the police find her friends.

Seren's dad must have driven quite fast from South Wales because he arrives in office 409 having taken only 2 hours 35 minutes to get there. He walks up to Seren, who is still sat at the table and gives her a long cwtch. "Dad you are squashing me!" muffles Seren into his chest. "You had me so worried Seren, but I am also secretly impressed you managed to make it all the way here on your own. Don't tell your mam I said that though," he says winking at her and then smiling.

Garry takes a seat with everyone around the big round table. "Thank you for looking after Seren, Dr Shaw," he says turning to look at the woman sat next to him. Dr Shaw fills in Garry on what has happened in Svalbard and their plans to go there to help with the search. She says she will keep them both informed on what happens out there and then suggests they leave now to get back on the road to Wales to beat the traffic starting up again.

"No!" Seren blurts out. She pulls down on her dad's arm as he goes to stand up from his seat. "Dr Shaw I can help; you must take me to Svalbard with you!"

"Oh Seren, don't be so silly. I know you want to help find Dr Owen, but you have done all you can do," says Garry softly to his daughter.

"Dad, I can ask Milo what happened, you know I can. He can tell me where the bad man took everyone. I can find out where they went. You know I can!" Seren screeches hysterically.

It takes quite a lot of effort to calm Seren down and Garry leaves her playing with a pop-it fidget toy that Juliet found on one of the other PhD student's desks. He and Dr Shaw go into her office to discuss Seren's abilities. Luckily, Seren's Dad can be very persuasive. He once convinced a car company in the South Wales valleys to take on ten apprentice mechanics, when they originally said they absolutely, definitely, could not take on any more than three!

Dr Shaw and Garry both reappear, and Dr Shaw sits down next to Seren. "Your father has explained to me your abilities, and the scientist part of me is struggling to believe you can do this: communicate with dogs? I mean, it sounds crazy."

Dr Shaw pauses and furrows her brow, thinking to herself seriously for a few moments before speaking again.

"But I do know that in science, and with the human mind in particular, there is a lot we still do not understand. And I really want to do everything in my power to find my friends and get them back safely. I am going to get Juliet to book us all on the next flight to Svalbard. I've suggested to your dad that he drives you both down to the big shopping centre in Southampton to buy you some more warm weather clothing; I'll use my budget to pay for your extra clothes and the flights, don't worry."

Seren is so relieved that Dr Shaw doesn't think she's making up her abilities, and that she trusts that she can help them.

"Thank you for believing in me Dr Shaw, I won't let you down," responds Seren hopefully.

Chapter 11

The next morning Seren, her dad, Dr Shaw and Juliet are all in contemplative silence as they walk into Departures at Southampton airport. They just checked in their suitcases at the Norwegian Air desk. Seren and her dad had to buy new suitcases yesterday; Seren is still upset the only ones they could find were both black, now her case will just look just like everyone else's; boring. When Garry rang Stella last night, she was very shocked to hear that both her daughter and husband would not only be staying overnight in Southampton, but they would then be getting on plane to Norway! "I am not sure how long we will be there, hopefully only a few days," said Seren's dad, trying to ease his wife's worries and failing miserably.

Anyway, the four are about to board their first plane of three. The first one, a small propeller plane, will only get them as far as Amsterdam Airport. They then need to change again in Tromsø (which Dr Shaw informed Seren is in mainland Norway) and then finally they will land in Svalbard by 8pm that night.

Seren is in for a long day of travelling.

When Seren finally steps off the plane in Svalbard airport wearing her purple puffer coat and yellow bobble hat, she feels very grateful for those two extra thermal layers she bought in the shopping centre. She actually put on all her layers on the final flight, in the aeroplane toilet. Sadly, the outdoor shop didn't have any children's thermal layers in purple, but they did have nice teal ones, and teal is Seren's third favourite colour, with yellow being her second. Seren was quite warm for those last 30 minutes of the plane journey though. Her Dad said she was being "a bit silly" putting her thermal layers on while they were still on the plane, but as she looks over at him shivering in just one layer, his yellow jacket, as he walks down the plane stairs she can't help but giggle to herself.

After the group successfully get through passport control, they collect their bags from the carousel and come out into Arrivals. Eventually they spot a large, stocky man with blonde hair and square shaped face holding a white sign scrawled with 'Dr Shaw' in capital letters and red pen.

"I am Dr Shaw. You must be our driver? We need to get to the police station in Longyearbyen as quickly as possible please."

"Ok, not a problem. My name is Lars Andersen. Can I take anyone's bags?" says the driver as reaches out for the biggest bag, which is Juliet's.

In the taxi, everyone else seems quiet and lost in their own thoughts, so Seren takes the opportunity to quiz Lars all about his life in Svalbard. "Lars do you get depressed in the winter living here? I saw a YouTube that said you don't see the Sun for almost three months here, and you call it 'Polar Night' because it's always nighttime!" she asks enthusiastically, catching Lars' eye in the rearview mirror from her position in the back, middle seat.

"I have lived here for over ten years now," replies Lars smiling, his eyes meeting Seren's momentarily in the rearview mirror. "I am used to the Polar Night now, I quite like the darkness because you can be all cozy by the fire and I can put on my candles and read a book and watch the flames flickering, and I can do this at any time of the day. We call this feeling of coziness 'Hygge', and I am a big fan of hygge myself! I actually find it harder to live here in the summer with twenty-four hours of daylight. You really feel the pressure to be outside all the time then. I always feel like I need to make the most of the three months of the sunlight, before it disappears again. I get quite stressed out trying to pack in lots of outdoor activities around doing my job. So, yeah, I don't get depressed at this time of year, I love me some darkness and hygge."

"Do you like your job? I bet you get to meet all sorts of people?" asks Seren.

"I don't mind being a taxi driver, but I've only actually done this job for a few months. I used to work in the coal mine, and to be honest I much preferred that. I had lots of miner friends." Lars seems lost in his memories, and then he says, "The mine is high up on the mountain. You can't see the mountain very well at the moment, but it's up there." Lars points into the vast darkness. "As someone who likes the dark and working with their hands, being a miner, it suited me just fine. Mining coal was how most people earned money here in Svalbard, but last month they closed down the last of the mines, and all the miners lost their jobs. A lot of the miners were like me, mining is the only job we have ever known. So, a lot of us struggled to get new jobs. I consider myself lucky to have this job. And you are right, I get to meet lots of nice people just like you." Lars gives Seren a wink in the rear-view mirror.

At this point Seren's dad decides to join the conversation, "Sorry to hear about the mines Lars. Seren and I are from South Wales and there used to be lots of mines there too, although, those ones all closed down back in the nineties. What was the main reason for closing the ones here in Longyearbyen?" asks Garry.

"Well, the Norwegian government want to move away from using coal. They want to reduce their carbon emissions and put more money into renewable energy. Here in Svalbard, we have a lot of different animals, and it's hard for them to live in such extreme conditions. The glaciers are melting of course, so there is a real concern about how burning coal effects them and our local environment."

Lars goes quiet again, lost in his thoughts, "It makes sense that it had to close, but it is hard for people here on the islands because the only other places to get work is at the university or in tourism."
Lars slows the car to a stop, "Anyway, here we are folks, that's the police station up ahead," he says pointing at the dark building ahead of them.

Seren can just about make out the word 'Politistasjonen' above two massive blue double doors. As she steps out of the car behind her dad she looks beyond the building into the sky. She still can't get over how dark it is here; how dark everything is in Svalbard. Sure, it is 9pm, so her brain is expecting darkness, but this is the darkest dark she's ever witnessed; it's on a totally new level. The sky certainly seems much darker than the sky she sees from her back garden in the valleys of South Wales.

As Seren walks towards the police station, still looking up at the sky, she thinks to herself that she probably should have listened to her nan and eaten more carrots. Every time her Nan makes them a roast dinner on a Sunday she says, "make sure you eat up all of them carrots Seren, it will help you see in the dark!" Extra night vision would be good in this place.

The Politistasjonen is very bright inside, and this is quite a shock given the sheer darkness of the outside. The white walls reflect the many overhead strip lights, so as the group walk into the main reception all four are blinking and covering their eyes as they adjust to onslaught. The receptionist also appears to be called Lars; it must be a popular name here in Norway. He's also tall and blonde, but not as chatty as Driver Lars, he just leads them into a large room with green plastic chairs and says, "Wait here. Detective Dorritt Santelmann and Detective Noah Broch are dealing with the case of the missing space physicists and the radar engineer. I will send them right in to speak with you."

Dr Shaw, Seren, her dad, and Juliet all take a seat on the squeaky chairs and stare at the bare, white walls. Seren hates any type of silence normally and would fill it straight away by telling everyone some facts she knows, but even she cannot think of anything to say. The weight of everyone's worries makes the air in the small waiting room feel thick and heavy. The confirmation from the police that their friends are indeed missing has made it all seem too real. Seren tries to stop herself thinking about how incredibly scared they must all be, wherever they are?

Chapter 12

When Detective Dorritt finally enters the room, Seren finds herself staring at her long, thick, wavy, ginger hair tied back into a ponytail. Seren wishes her hair was as long and thick as Detective Dorritt's, and then she starts to wonder how she, Seren, would look with ginger hair.

Detective Noah, who walks in just after Detective Dorritt, has strawberry-blonde hair, which is also quite long, also in a ponytail, he has a bit of ginger stubble, but not enough for it to be a proper beard.

After some formal introductions, Detective Dorritt sits down next to Seren and says to her seriously, "I understand you saw the kidnapping on a video call with Dr Owen? Can you give me a description of any of the kidnappers."

"The one I saw had a balaclava on," answers Seren, "so I don't know what he looked like. It all happened so fast. I think he was a man, and he had an accent, a bit like Driver Lars, who drove us here. He had on a black hoodie too, I remember that. There might have been another voice that I heard just before the call cut off, it wasn't Charlie or Dr Dan's voice. I guess it could have been the engineer though, I never got to speak to him, so I don't know what he sounds like."

"Ok, thanks Seren, that's useful information," says Detective Dorritt. Seren notices that the detective is smiling and thinks this is a bit of a strange reaction, especially because Seren couldn't tell her much at all about what the kidnappers looked like, or how many there were.

Before Detective Dorritt can turn to question the adults, Seren suddenly jumps in, "Where is Milo Detective Dorritt? If I can see Milo, I might be able to get some more information for you?"

Dorritt turns away from Seren to Dr Shaw with a look of utter confusion, and before Seren can explain any further, Dr Shaw asks to speak with Detective Dorritt in a private room. Both women leave and then Detective Noah, who is sitting next to

Garry, says, "as Seren's dad I was wondering if you were witness to the call? Maybe you remember something?" Garry looks embarrassed and responds slowly, "I did see the start of the call, but then I fell asleep, so I didn't see any of the kidnapping. Sorry, Seren's got this amazing armchair in her bedroom, and it really is rather comfy."

When Detective Dorritt and Dr Shaw come back into the room, it is clear their conversation hasn't gone very well; both women look angry and stressed. However, Dorritt, while looking sceptical, asks them all to follow her to staff room where Milo is. Detective Noah explains that because the engineer, Austen, lives alone and the rest of his family are in Norway, on the mainland, there was no one to take care of Milo at such short notice. Instead, one of the police dog handlers took him home last night and brought him back into work today.

The group enter the staff room. Seren thinks it has more personality than the last room. There are posters on the wall and a few comfortable looking blue leather chairs, as opposed to the green hard plastic seats in the other room. Detective Noah points out the husky in the corner.

Milo, who, when Seren last saw him was sleeping soundly under the control room desk, is now shaking and wide eyed looking around the room frantically, left and right. His black and white ears are flat to his head and his tail is tight between his legs, one of his eyes is red with blood from burst vessels.

"Oh my gosh," cries Seren going straight over to the sad old husky dog and kneeling beside him, "what did they do to you Milo?"

Detective Noah fills them in on what happened. "We think Milo tried to attack the kidnappers. He would have tried to protect Austen, and based on his injuries it seems they might have kicked him in the head. They could have kicked him so hard that he passed out, which explains why he didn't chase after them, and why when we found him, he was still inside the control room."

"Awww Milo," responds Seren, stroking his fur softly. Milo looks up into her eyes, he seems to be pleading for her to help him.

"Please can you all leave me alone with Milo. I want to help, and I think it will be easier if it is just me and him." Seren announces, shooing everyone from the room.

Detective Noah, the only one who hasn't been told about Seren's abilities, looks to the others to explain; he has no idea how leaving a ten-year-old with a husky dog is going to help. Detective Dorritt, who hasn't moved from inside the entrance door to the staff room, sees his confusion and gestures with her hand for them to all move toward the door. "We will just be outside in the corridor if you need us Seren," Dorritt says with a cynical tone to her voice, as they all leave the room.

Seren continues to stroke Milos long grey-black fur. She wants to make sure he is comfortable with her before she attempts to communicate with him.

Finally, after lots of stroking and reassurance from Seren his large body stops shaking and he seems calm. Seren places her hand very lightly on the top of his head fur and then says out loud, "Milo, what happened to Austen? Can you help us find him? Who hurt you?"

She waits.

After a few moments of sitting in silence she can sense bursts of images coming through from Milo. These flashes of information seem to suggest there were two kidnappers: the big man with the balaclava that was in the office with Dr Owen and told her to hang up the call, and another smaller man who Milo saw leading Charlie and Dr Dan out of the control room. The smaller man was holding a knife at their backs. It seems Austen got caught off-guard coming out of the toilet by the bigger man. On seeing Austen coming out of the toilet the bad man slammed his elbow upwards into Austen's nose. While Austen was clutching his face in shock from the blow, the bad man punched him in the stomach, and then pushed him back into the toilet against the door.

Milo did manage to bite the bigger man on the ankle, but then something, maybe a boot, hit Milo's face, the blow was so hard he passed out. He doesn't remember anything after that, but he was probably kicked again in the stomach because his ribs really hurt.

Seren can sense how reliving the memory of Austen being taken has made Milo really very upset. "It's ok Milo," says Seren reassuringly rubbing his head fur, "you did your best to stop them, they sound like very bad men, not just for the kidnapping bit, but for kicking you in the head bit too. People who hurt animals are just the worst. I just keep thinking about how sad and angry I would be if someone ever kicked Bili!"

After a few moments where Seren is just massaging Milo's head she starts to 'hear' more of his thoughts down the connection.

"I just feel so old and useless Seren," says Milo. "I don't even have a good sense of smell anymore. I don't think I could follow the scent of the kidnapper, even though I bit his ankle. Thankfully, I do know Austen's scent, of course. I just don't understand why the police haven't taken me back up to the radar to at least try pick up the direction that Austen was taken; I can smell him for sure. I'm desperate to help Seren, and I miss Austen so much. I'm really worried. Like you said, those were such bad, cruel men that took him."

"Thank you for sharing all that with me, Milo," says Seren, looking into the husky's sad grey eyes very seriously. She pauses and strokes her hand down his head onto his back fur. "I am going to go tell everyone what happened straight away. I will do all I can to explain how we need you to track Austen's scent and find out where they were taken."

Chapter 13

The group, minus Detective Noah, are driven up the mountain road to the EISCAT radar station in the police's large four-wheel drive vehicle. It's a massive car, but Detective Dorritt insisted that Noah stay in the station and finish paperwork instead of joining them. Seren thought it was a bit weird that Detective Dorritt didn't want her partner to join them, but the drive up to the radar station was so mesmerising with the snow-capped mountains on either side, that she soon forgot about Detective Noah. Her brain was filled of thoughts of how amazing this place is, and how it's a shame she's not visiting for more fun reasons.

As the group step out of the large vehicle and close the car doors behind them, they all look up in wonder at the immense radars rising out of the seemingly never-ending blanket of snow.

This first sighting of the radar on arrival in Svalbard, it normally fills Dr Shaw and Juliet with such excitement for all the research data they will get to collect. But now, this place just feels tainted because of all that has happened, now it is the place where their friends were kidnapped. How they wish the only mysteries they had to unravel was that of the mysterious aurora.

"It's so cool you and Austen get to hang out here at the radar station all the time, Milo!" Seren says enthusiastically to Milo as she walks next to him toward the radar entrance door. She is trying to cheer him up, but she instantly regrets the mention of Austen because Milo starts to shake again. The husky dog leads the group through the entrance door of the EISCAT radar station, between two large, looming radar.

Inside the control room Detective Dorritt shows everyone where the kidnapping took place. She points out the damage to the toilet door where Austen fell on it and shows them under the desk where they found Milo. As she walks them into the office where Dr Owen was at the end of the call with Seren, she goes on to say, "of course, we don't know how many kidnappers there were."

Seren quickly corrects her. "There were two kidnappers Detective Dorritt. Milo told me that there were two, and I told you. So, we do know that!"

Detective Dorritt doesn't even acknowledge that Seren has spoken, and Seren is noticeably upset by being ignored.

Garry, seeing his daughter distraught, responds sternly, "regardless of your lack of belief Detective Dorritt, we should still make as much use of Seren and Milo's connection. Milo wants to try to see if he can smell Austen's scent. We should at least try to see what direction they were taken. As far as I am aware you don't even have a search party looking for the scientists. I am honestly surprised the police haven't made use of Milo already. Using a dog's ability to track their human with their superior sense of smell is pretty obvious, in my opinion!"

Detective Dorritt looks taken aback, and she is clearly lost for words to retaliate. Silently she leads the group outside, to the back of the building, where there is a steep bank of snow. Milo instantly puts his nose down to the snowy ground and starts moving his head side to side taking deep sniffs. Meanwhile, Dr Shaw turns to Detective Dorritt, "If Milo does manage to find a scent in a certain direction, how will we go about following it? The snow looks so thick in all directions. Is there even a road that goes higher up the mountain from here?" asks Dr Shaw.

"Indeed, this is the problem," Dorritt says, eyeing Garry who is still scowling at her. "The road is only ploughed from Longyearbyen up to this radar station. It used to be ploughed much further, all the way up to the coal mine which is high on the Breinosa mountain," she points toward a large mountain peak in the south-east. "But now the mine is closed, there's no need to get the coal down the mountain, so there is no need to plough the snow any further than this." She pauses, trudging further up the bank.

"The scientists at the Kjell Henriksen Observatory, which is about one kilometre north of this radar station, they have to use a military tank to get up there. The tank has big tracks on it that can handle the thick snow. It was gifted to the University of Svalbard from the Norwegian army to allow the scientists to get up to the observatory from the radar without the need of the plough. The tank needs to be booked by the scientists in advance if they need to go to the observatory because only a few people, like Austen the engineer, are trained to drive it. On the night your friends were kidnapped it seems the tank would have been parked outside the radar; Dr Dan Winter was scheduled to use one of the telescopes up there the following night. Given the fact the tank is no longer here, and it isn't at the observatory, we assume the kidnappers stole the tank to allow them to travel into the mountains," says Detective Dorritt.

"I see," replies Dr Shaw. "I assume it's unlikely they would take the tank toward the observatory as then they might have been seen by the scientists who are staying up there. So, we can probably rule out that direction?"

"Well, I don't think we can rule out anything at this stage," answers Dorritt sternly, "the snow fall we had yesterday was so heavy it would have filled in the deep tank tracks, so they really could be anywhere!" Seren can see from just her dad's facial expressions that he is really not a fan of Detective Dorritt.

"Surely it's better to choose the most likely option and start searching in that direction though, rather than just doing nothing!" responds Garry angrily.

Chapter 14

As the grown-ups continue to bicker about what the police should be doing, Seren goes over to where Milo is sniffing at the deep snow. She notices that he does seem to be moving less side to side and more in a specific direction. "Are you picking up Austen's scent Milo?" Seren questions him, kneeling down next to him and stroking the rough fur on Milo's back. Seren doesn't even need to use her abilities to understand, the husky answers very clearly by bringing his head up from the ground and pointing his snout with purpose towards the mountains in the east. His eyes seem to bulge out of his head as if saying, 'That way!' Seren quickly realises that this is the direction that Dorritt pointed out when she was describing where the coal mine is, the Breinosa mountain.

"Milo can smell Austen in this direction!" shouts Seren to the grown-ups, pointing south-east towards the mountain. "Do you think the kidnappers could be keeping them at the coal mine?" Seren asks as the grown-ups walk over to her and Milo.

Detective Dorritt is the first to get to Seren and Milo, she is still looking very moody and sceptical. "The coal mine is closed Seren, but it still has security guards who check it, so I don't think it's realistic that they would be able to keep captives there without someone realising." Dorritt lets out a long sigh, then turns to the adults, "I am not inclined to choose our search direction based on the nose of this old dog, that does nothing but sleep under a desk all day, and a ten-year-old who thinks she can hear the thoughts of dogs!" shouts Dorritt, her Norwegian accent getting thicker the angrier she gets.

"Well, I disagree," says Dr Shaw, she already feels very protective of Seren. "I think arranging a search of the coal mine would be a great place to start; we have to start somewhere. Our colleagues have been missing for more than three days and I really don't understand why you haven't yet started searching for them Detective!"

Seren's dad and Juliet both nod in agreement. "Do the police have a mode of transport that can get to the coal mine?" asks Juliet.

"The four-wheel drive car we came up in can get up there, I guess. We would have to put the big snow chains on the tyres though. Unfortunately, I left the snow chains down at the station," answers Detective Dorritt.

"This is absolutely ridiculous!" shouts Garry, looking around at the other grown-ups in disbelief. His face is all scrunched up, this is the look Seren's mam calls 'The Face'. When her dad has this look, Seren knows not to ask him any more questions for at least 30 minutes. When he has 'The Face' it means he is very stressed and needs time to calm down.

"Four people have been missing for more than three days and you aren't doing anything about it. It seems like you just can't be bothered to help us search for them!" Garry yells at Dorritt. Both are looking very red in the face now.

"I will not be spoken to like this anymore," Detective Dorritt shouts back. She turns around dramatically and storms around the outside of the building, her thick black boots making deep imprints in the snow.

Before the group can process what is happening, they hear the car's engine starting up and see powdery snow being blown up behind the vehicle as Detective Dorritt wheel spins their only mode of transport away down the mountain.

"She just left us here?" asks Seren in disbelief, her large hazel eyes looking up to Dr Shaw and then across to her dad for reassurance.

"That does seem to be the case Seren," says Dr Shaw sounding and looking shocked, "but don't worry, we have everything we need here in the control room building. People can stay up here for a few days if they need to do a long radar run. It has a kitchen, dining area and even a few pull-out beds. Let's all go and have a sit down in the kitchen with a nice cup of tea and discuss our next steps, shall we?" Dr Shaw suggests to the group, trying her best to sound calm. But everyone can tell she is very worried about their change in circumstances and that she is just trying to put on a brave face. She leads the group through the deep snow back into the warmth and safety of the building.

Chapter 15

Detective Dorritt has never driven so fast in all her time in the police force, even when driving to an emergency with her blue lights flashing. She just had to get out of there! She's so enraged by that ridiculous child who thinks she can speak with dogs, not to mention her interfering father. It makes her think about her own father. He too used to be so passionate; he always had her back; he would always stand up for her. He used to be so proud of her and tell everyone about her work in the police force, he was especially proud when she got promoted to detective. He was always so interested in her work and would ask her lots of questions about it whenever she would visit him, now she can barely get a word out of him.

Her father was a coal miner, and he really loved his job. You could tell it really gave him a real sense of purpose and he was always such a confident man because of the pride he had in being a miner. That coal mine provided most of the energy needs for everyone in Svalbard, so it was important work. He always loved chatting with people, even tourists and university students, he regularly socialised with the other miners, but ever since he lost his job in the mine he doesn't want to chat with anyone. The moment they closed that mine down, it seems all his joy in life was left deep under the ground, in the dark, with all that coal. His work was his identity and now that's gone… he's lost.

Dorritt arrives on the outskirts of the Longyearbyen settlement in record time, without realising, but probably because she was so angry thinking about her poor father, she has driven right up to her father's house. She turns the engine off and smacks the steering wheel with her hands. Well, she is here now so she may as well check in on him. Besides, her colleagues at the police station think that she is up at the radar so she can't go back there yet. As she gets out of the car she wonders to herself how best to explain that she just drove off and abandoned the people she is supposed to be helping. "Oh well," Dorritt says to herself, "I can figure that out later."

Dorritt lived in this house with her father and her Farmor up until she became a detective two years ago (Farmor is the Norwegian word for Nan). The house is so full of memories, and the decoration hasn't changed at all since her mother passed away. Dorritt's mother died of breast cancer when Dorritt was only three years old, so she doesn't really remember her; she only knows what her mother looks like from the faded family photos that still cover the beige walls. She knows she had thick ginger hair like hers and that her big green eyes 'are just like her mothers'. Dorritt is an only child, and after her mother died her Farmor moved in and raised her.

Farmor was also her best friend. Dorritt told her everything, and she misses her so much; especially since she doesn't have any friends at the police station. As far as her dad is concerned, she moved out because of her promotion to detective, but really it was because her Farmor died. She couldn't face living there with just him, without her. Between her dad losing his job at the coal mine and her Farmor dying, life has just felt so hard recently. Whenever

Dorritt visits her father, she always leaves feeling really depressed. Nevertheless, she always visits him at least once a week. Her dad has no one else.

Her father, like many of the miners, is too proud to look for another job. To him, being a miner, wasn't just a job it was his whole way of life.

"Hallo!" says Dorritt, as she opens the front door trying to sound as enthusiastic and joyful as she can manage.

"Don't be getting snow on my carpet Dorritt!" her father shouts from the living room.

"Nice to see you too Dad," Dorritt says quietly under her breath as she removes her boots and walks inside to see her father sitting in his usual spot. He looks back at her from his upright position in the grey, high-backed chair, as usual he has a newspaper folded on top of his red, wool blanket that sits over his lap.

Dorritt looks through to the kitchen behind him and sees dirty dishes and mugs covering all the surfaces. Everywhere, there is a thick covering of dust, and the cream carpet is littered with empty food containers.

"How are you doing?" asks Dorritt, sitting on the old cream leather sofa opposite, trying to make eye contact with her father. He just stares at the window, with its grimy net curtain. He takes a sip from the beer in his hand and Dorritt thinks he is going to speak but he just keeps staring at the window. As Dorritt ponders what she might say to get her dad to respond, she feels her phone vibrating in her pocket. Assuming it's the police station, she automatically moves her finger over the red symbol to hang up, but then she sees the words 'Skurk calling'.

'Why on earth does he want?' thinks Dorritt, 'he knows I am technically on duty right now.' Dorritt stands, leaving her father, she walks back out into the corridor. She paces back and for in an anxious panic as she decides whether to answer the phone to Skurk.

Chapter 16

Inside the control room kitchen, the group sit squashed together around a small, round table that is only designed to seat three people. Luckily Seren and Milo don't take up too much room. Each of the group is holding a matching mug, patterned with polar bears, outlined in blue; even Milo's bowl under the table has polar bears on it. Seren is finding a lot of pleasure in the fact that they all take their tea the same way: a dash of milk and no sugar.

To try and break the tension of the moment, Juliet explains to Seren and her dad that the people of Svalbard love polar bears so much that they put them on everything. "They are even the logo for the supermarket," she says. Pointing out the logo on the front of her dark blue hoodie she adds, "everything here in Svalbard is really expensive, especially the souvenirs for the tourists, but in the supermarket, you can buy their branded hoodies with the polar bear logo on. My friends think it's a bit weird; I wear this hoodie all the time at home, they say it's like having a hoodie with 'Lidl' on it, but the logo is so cool don't you think?" By this point, Seren is bouncing in her chair, she does this a lot when she is trying to listen to someone talking but is also very excited to share a fact with them. Her mam always has to remind her not to interrupt people with her facts, Seren must at least wait until they have finished speaking. She figures that because Juliet asked her a question, then it's finally ok for her to speak, so she stops bouncing.

"I do love your hoodie Juliet; I wonder if they have it in purple. And yes, it does makes sense that they love polar bears so much here; I read online that there are more polar bears living in Svalbard than people, there are 2,500 people and 3,000 polar bears!" Seren says proudly.

Seren's Dad smiles at his daughter. He's always amazed at her ability to retain information, and he loves seeing her excitement for sharing her knowledge with others. Garry thinks that Seren reminds him of himself when he was young, he used to love searching through his encyclopaedia books for facts to wow his parents and friends with; his favourite thing to read about when he was ten years old was dinosaurs. In this moment he takes strength from watching his daughter talk; from seeing her eagerness to learn and to help others, and from how she seems to lift the spirits of those she talks to.

Seren's dad moves his strong hands around his mug and takes a big sip of tea. Everyone copies him and takes a sip, and as the warm liquid enters their bodies, it seems to fill everyone up with something truly powerful: hope.

Garry looks across to Dr Shaw with his smile now so big that the lines around his eyes are creasing, and he says, "So, how long is the walk to the mine?" Dr Shaw smiles back at him. She looks so relieved. She wasn't bold enough to suggest to the group that they could hike up to the mine and start the search themselves.

"The mine is about ten kilometres away," she answers. "It will be slow going because the snow will be very deep in places, but I think we have enough pairs of snowshoes and crampons here. We even have a small set that Seren can use; one of the climate scientists who comes up here regularly has very small feet!"

Seren jumps up from her chair, almost knocking both her chair and the remains of her tea over. "Ok, let's get going then!" she says to the group, looking around at everyone, "how long will it take us to get there, Dr Shaw?"

Dr Shaw looks at Juliet, then back at Seren before she replies. "Seren, I admire your eagerness and your bravery, but we need to sit here for a while and plan this all out. We mustn't be hasty. The last thing we want is to end up on the side of the mountain, unprepared and needing to be rescued ourselves." Dr Shaw pauses, "Juliet," she says, turning to her for a moment. Juliet sits forward, eager, ready to help. "I need you go find the map and our GPS system and I'll start preparing some food and drinks to take with us."

Juliet stands up from the table, but just before she leaves the kitchen Dr Shaw adds, "and Juliet, while you are in the cupboard can you check we have enough snowshoes and crampons for everyone."

Dr Shaw turns back to the table, "Seren, you and your dad should check you each have enough layers of clothing; if you haven't, tell us what you need, and we can check the lost and found box."

Dr Shaw moves towards a large cupboard in the corner, opening the door to reveal a laundry-type box stuffed full of clothes. "As you can see it's overflowing with stuff, and it's still about minus twenty degrees outside right now so we need to make sure we are all wrapped up warm. I will also need to check there aren't any storms coming in, I'll go do that on my laptop in a sec. Assuming the weather is ok, and we can go at a good walking pace it should take us about four to five hours to get to the coal mine. It is, of course, going to be very, very dark so we will all need head torches, but luckily, we have spares of those here too. And don't worry, Juliet and I have been trained to use the flare guns in the case we come across a polar bear. They get scared away by the noise and the light from the flare going off."

Seren momentarily ponders what it might be like to see a polar bear in real life, and then she snaps back to the matter at hand. "Will Milo be able to come with us?" asks Seren as she kneels and strokes the back of the confused looking husky sprawled on the kitchen floor tiles.

Dr Shaw replies, "I am so sorry, Seren, he is just too old." Milo looks up at them both with a heavy sadness in his blue eyes. "I know it will be disappointing for him, but we will be able to walk much quicker without him. I don't think he walks much further than one kilometre each day with Austen, and then he just sleeps and, especially with his injuries, it wouldn't be fair on him."

As Seren moves her hand to the dog's head and concentrates on his thoughts, she can tell he is indeed upset, but he accepts that Dr Shaw is right. "He understands," says Seren, looking around the room at everyone. "I just hope we can bring Austen back to Milo safely."

Chapter 17

In a mysterious and dark location somewhere in Svalbard, the kidnapped Astronomy Outreach Leader, Dr Julie Owen stirs and wipes the drool from the side of her cheek. She is very surprised, but very grateful that she has finally managed to get some sleep. She's slept in some uncomfortable locations in her thirty-nine years of life: on a deflated air mattress while hiking in Patagonia; at the Glastonbury music festival where she worked in the science tent; and on the floor of an observatory in Chile in between collecting data on supernova stars. But on the cold hard floor of this cell, that has to be the worst. She looks over at Dr Dan and Charlie who are both sitting up and leaning against the dark walls of their small cell, clutching thick blankets to themselves.

"How are you doing?" Dr Dan asks Dr Owen, as she sits up against the wall and moves away the hair that is sticking to her face.

"I've felt better," she says, attempting to smile but failing. "Do you know what time it is, Dan? My Fitbit died, and I've lost all sense of time."

The cell that encases the scientists has four walls; two are the corner of a large cavern with dark, angular rocks jutting out, and the other two walls are formed from thick metal bars about 6cm apart. The two walls made from the metal bars have been attached to the corner walls with big, thick bolts. The scientist's cell is one of two that have been built into the corners of the dark cavern. However, the other cell does not contain human prisoners. Instead, the other cell contains three massive, but frail looking polar bears.

Given the state of the polar bears; how skinny and quiet they are, and the dirty colour of their fur, the scientists assume they have been there for much longer than them.

"It's 10.30pm now. I can't believe we have been here, what, almost four days?" Dr Dan sighs. "They brought us some food and water about this time

126

yesterday; I hope they bring us some more today, I'm so hungry."

From the corner of the cavern where there is an opening onto a long, rocky walled corridor, the group hear footsteps getting louder. Out of the dim light steps a tall man wearing a thick black coat and black balaclava. In his hands is a tray containing a large bowl of porridge with a single spoon sticking out of it, and around the bowl, on the tray three plastic bottles of water roll around. He puts the tray onto the hard floor and then unlocks the door to the cell before sliding the tray quickly inside. As he locks the door the man glares in at scientists. Charlie asks, "Why are you keeping us in here? We are just a group of aurora scientists. What possible reason could you have for keeping us here?" The man in the balaclava ignores Charlie, just as he has on all the other occasions when he asked him the same question.

Turning his back on the scientists, the balaclava man walks quickly out of the cavern along the long rocky corridor into a small room, it has a very bright lamp in the corner, but it is also somehow dark and gloomy, like the cavern he just left. Totally covering one of the walls of the room are five large computer screens, one shows a live feed of the sky above Svalbard, another shows images of glaciers, and the others have many different graphs, all relating to Svalbard's climate.

In front of the wall of screens, another, bigger man sits at a long desk, hunched over a laptop. He is frantically typing away but stops as his balaclava wearing friend comes into the room.

"He's still trying to make out that they are just aurora scientists, Skule," says the smaller man as he takes his balaclava off and drops it onto the desk next to a closed laptop.

"He's lying to you. He's just saying anything he can think of, so we let them go," replies the bigger man, angrily. "Idiot, they are climate scientists. I won't tell you this again: you can't trust them. And don't use my real name. I know they probably can't hear us in here, but this whole place is very echoey, and if

I end up in jail because of your stupidity I will take you down with me. I call you 'Idiot' and you just call me 'Skurk'."

Chapter 18

Seren rolls over on her thin mattress on the radar control room floor and taps her dad on his shoulder. He is still sleeping soundly on the mattress next to her. "Wake up Dad, we need to save the scientists," she says to him softly.

Yesterday was such a long day for them; three flights to get to Svalbard from Southampton and then after a fight to convince the police to help them, they are then abandoned on the side of a mountain.

By the time Dr Shaw and Juliet had packed up everything they needed for their hike to the mine yesterday, it was close to midnight. Dr Shaw suggested it would be best for them all to try and get a good six hours of sleep before they ventured out in the snow in search of their friends. Plus, it made more sense to wait until the morning, specifically 7am because it was clear from the weather radar that the 'precipitation percentage' was going to drop off at that time. Seren would have stayed up all night quizzing Juliet about how the GPS and weather radar worked. She especially liked saying 'precipitation percentage' over and over, just because of the way it sounded, and she even kept saying it to herself in her head while she lay on her floor mattress, when she was supposed to be going to sleep. Just at the moment when her dad had started drifting off next to her she loudly announces to him, "Dad, did you know another name for snow and rain is 'precipitation'. I am so happy that the percentage likelihood of precipitation is going down from 70% to 30% at 7am tomorrow." Luckily Seren's dad is used to his daughter's sudden fact outbursts at inappropriate times, and he just whispers quietly to her, "good night, Seren."

~~~

After a traditional Norwegian breakfast of rye bread and cheese, and a cup of tea of course, the group start to layer up for their hike. Seren giggles to herself as she puts on an adult size merino wool, long sleeved top and trousers from the lost and found box, followed by her two layers that she bought in Southampton. She then puts on an odd pair of woolly socks (one is yellow, and one is blue). Dr Shaw picked these out of the box for her because they had both shrunk in the wash and are now the perfect size for a ten-year old's feet. Seren doesn't mind wearing odd socks, she wears her socks odd more often than matching, she finds it less boring to be odd.

After her dad helps her roll up the arms and legs on the borrowed layers so they aren't drooping over her hands and feet, she puts on her iconic purple puffer coat and yellow bobble hat. "Well, I am ready to go, just need my boots on," Seren announces, looking down at herself and patting down her coat.

"Seren, you look like the Michelin Man," laughs her dad, as he fastens his yellow coat up over his own layers.

"What's the Michelin Man, Dad? You are so silly!" Seren scolds her dad. "Anyway, we need to focus. Dr Shaw, do you have the GPS and the back-up paper map? I am happy to carry the paper map. I love maps!" she pauses, thinking about her favourite map on her wall at home. It's probably the map of the Canary Islands. She shakes herself back to focusing. "Now, let's hope the precipitation percentage is nice and low outside, below thirty percent would be ideal." Seren says this in her best 'scientist' voice as she saunters towards the door in her many, many layers of clothing.

The group manage to leave the EISCAT radar building heading south-east toward the coal mine in the Adventdalen valley by 7.45am, so they were running a bit late. Before they left, Juliet made sure to leave out some food and water out for Milo and she wrote a quick note of explanation for the climate scientists who are scheduled to use the radar tonight.

After the first 3 kilometres of walking, everything seems to be going to plan. The GPS computer is keeping them on track, telling them how far they have gone and where they are. The group are doing well, walking easily with their metal spiky 'crampons' attached over their hiking boots. Seren really enjoys the crunching sound the crampons make in the snow; she thinks it might even be better than running through crunchy leaves in the Autumn. As Seren crunches through the snow, she thinks about how much she would like to have a snowball fight, it would be so easy to pick up some snow, smooth it into a ball and throw it at her dad's back as she walks behind him. But she needs to focus, this is a serious rescue mission and there is not time for playing about.

As it approaches 11am and the group reach the halfway point in their hike, the darkness remains. It is dark in every direction, in all parts of the sky. The off-white of the mountains has no light to reflect, and all the sound is dampened, as if it should echo but it doesn't. It's eerie, but also so magical. High mountains rise out of the ground, on both sides, behind and ahead.

As Seren looks around her, thinking about how weird this cold, dark place is, some thick grey clouds start rolling over the mountain ahead. The sky once totally dark is now just totally grey with cloud. It changed so quickly. She calls out to Dr Shaw who leads the way. "Dr Shaw, I think the precipitation percentage just went up!" Seren points to the ominous looking nimbostratus clouds overhead.

Dr Shaw turns and calls back, "Yes, I think you are right Seren. Unfortunately predicting the weather is hard, just like predicting where and when the aurora will be visible."

Seren stops and waits for her dad to catch up to her. "Dad, it looks like we might get some precipitation in the form of snow!" she tells him, again using her best scientist voice.

"Don't worry, Seren, we are making good time," he replies. "We are halfway there, but perhaps we should make a quick stop soon to have a snack and a drink before the snow comes."

As the group spot some large black rocks amongst the vast snow, likely moved into position by the glaciers of the past, they decide the rocks are a perfect place to sit down for a snack. Juliet hands

Seren some food, more rye bread and cheese, and sits down on a rock to eat her own. Seren takes her food quickly over to her dad who is tucking into his already, "Dad, I need to speak to you, it's a serious matter and it means I can't eat my gross rye bread yet."

"Why not Seren, what's wrong?" he says. He looks around, as if sensing danger, before peering hard at Seren's face to see if her expression holds any clues.

Seren steps close and whispers into his ear. "I really need a wee, and I can't eat my food if I need a wee, but it's going to take me ages to get all these layers off so I can have my wee!"

Garry smiles, he's relieved that Seren's 'serious matter' is just that she needs a wee. "It's ok Seren, we aren't going anywhere, and we will all be busy eating our rye bread and cheese, so we won't be looking at you. I'll ask Juliet and Dr Shaw to make sure they look the other way. Let me hold onto your food, and you can go behind that bush over there and have a wee, you don't need to worry." He points to an arctic willow bush about 7 meters from the black rock he is sitting on.

After a bit of a tussle trying to figure out the best way to conceal herself behind the arctic willow Seren manages to wrestle off her purple coat over her many woolly layers. She moves from side to side, holding her coat in one hand, looking at the sloping snow and tries to figure out where best to put her coat on the ground so that she doesn't wee on it.

With no warning at all, a big gust of wind blows her coat out of her hand, and it dances higher up the slope. As she starts to chase it streams of powdery snow fall to the ground from the sky above her, and then a large gust of wind blasts the snow on the ground up into her face. The wind starts howling too, and all Seren can see is the white haze of snow all around her as her purple coat rolls further away.

After a few failed attempts Seren finally manages to successfully grab hold of her coat. "Got you!" she exclaims. Turning around, she expects to see her chosen wee bush just behind her.

The bush is gone.

Everything is white, and as Seren starts to look about her, powder is blown into her eyes with force. She spins around several times. She tries not to panic. In her head she is repeating reassuring words to herself, "this is just a snowstorm; it appeared very quickly, it will disappear just as quickly, any moment now."

Seren is all alone in the arctic snow.

Or is she...?

Chapter 19

Seren tries to remember every fact she can from all the survival videos she's watched on YouTube. As she thinks of all this survival advice, she gets really overwhelmed and she starts to panic; is it 'shelter' or 'water' that you should sort out first? She can't remember, and then she gets very anxious because she has neither shelter or water! This is really a rather scary situation that she has found herself in.

Seren tries to calm her breathing and closes her eyes. After three deep breaths, in through her nose and out through her mouth, like Mrs Davies makes her do in school when she gets stressed, she opens her eyes and makes the decision to ignore all of YouTube and just trust her mam's advice.

Her mam has moaned at her many times about wandering off when she gets distracted by something; it's usually because she has decided to stop and look at something shiny and exciting, the last time it happened it was a squirrel in the local park, it was just stood there on the path, holding a big nut. It was truly fascinating to watch. Much more interesting than watching where Seren's mam was walking and following her.

Her Mam always tells the story of how they lost her in Lidl when she was five, and when they found her, she was sitting on the floor in the fruit aisle, trying to juggle oranges, totally oblivious to the fact she had lost her parents and was totally alone. After that happened her Mam would always say, "as soon as you realise that you can't see me or your dad anywhere, you just sit down, like you did with the oranges in Lidl. You sit where you are and don't move and we will come and find you!"

Putting back on her purple coat and zipping it right up to her chin, Seren hopes with all her heart that her mam is right. She sits down as the cold snow blasts and howls at her. She is determined to stay exactly where she is, waiting for her dad find her.

After just a few moments of sitting in the snow getting a very cold bottom, Seren decides her mam's advice maybe doesn't need to be taken so literally when in the literal Arctic. So, she stands up and starts hopping backing forth on her feet, trying to keep warm. She smacks her hands into her bottom to try and warm it back up. Even as she hops, she makes sure she is staying exactly over the spot in the show she was just sitting on so that her mam can't get mad with her for moving.

Still hopping from one foot to another, Seren decides the next thing she should do to try to survive would be to call out to her dad's name. The wind howls extremely loudly, and she is starting to get very cold and scared.

Seren shouts with all the energy she has, all the way from deep in her belly, into the direction she thinks the wee bush is in. "Dad! I'm over here! Dad! Please come find me! I'm staying on the same spot for you to find me!" She takes a deep breath and then shouts again, "Dad, I'm lost! Dad, I'm over here!"

Shouting for her dad releases some of the pent-up emotion in her body, but she struggles to contain it leaking out of her eyes. In an attempt to stop her tears coming Seren takes another deep breath in, holds it for 3 seconds and then breathes out. She whispers out loud to herself, over and over, "it's going to be ok Seren."

She tries to imagine what her best friend India would say to her in this moment. India always knows what to say to cheer her up, sometimes she even knows Seren is upset before Seren knows herself. She imagines India next to her, whispering with confidence: "Seren you just need to trust yourself. You are so strong, and you have such long, beautiful eyelashes, and you are really good at maths, so don't you forget that!"

Seren continues to jump on the spot and has a little giggle to herself thinking about the funny stuff her best friend comes out with. Then, as she looks around, trying to pick out the nearest horizon, or anything that isn't snow in all directions, there opens a small gap in the falling snow.

Seren has a sense that someone is watching her.

Through the gap in the snow, she can see something moving. The something is white, and it moves quickly. It's breathing loudly. It can't be her dad because he isn't wearing white. He has a yellow coat on, and he doesn't move that quickly, especially in the snow.

"Hello?" Seren calls out.

Chapter 20

The white something has eyes. Eyes as black as the Arctic night, and they are looking right at Seren. Before she has time to even contemplate calling out to it again, it starts to move away from her, camouflaged. She tries to get a better look at it, at the back of the moving shape. The white, quick creature. It has a tail.

Seren is so scared. Her brain starts firing off lots of options for what this mystery creature could be, and she thinks up seven possible ways that it could attack her. Why does her brain always do this to her? Why is it always so full of thoughts and scenarios? Seren shakes her head from side to side trying to make her busy brain focus. She is indeed very frightened, but just before the mystery creature appeared she was also feeling so terribly and awfully alone. If Seren can get it to come back, then at least she will no longer be all on her own. She is probably the bravest she has ever been in her whole life when she shouts after the retreating white-tailed thing.

"Come back. I won't hurt you, please come back."

The creature seems to hear her because it stops moving away. It turns around and Seren sees those black eyes looking back at her through the falling snow. She nervously smiles at the creature. "What are you?" she wonders aloud.

Seren finds a courage from deep within in herself. Despite the adrenaline coursing through her veins telling her to run away, she remains still. In fact, Seren is still standing in the same place that she has been this whole time, like her mam told her to. The white creature pads toward her, slowly, keeping its dark eyes locked on hers.

Closer, closer, it comes. The snow is still falling fast around them, and the mysterious creature is only a few metres away from Seren before she realises what it is.

A polar bear.

Chapter 21

The polar bear is incredibly close now, their noses almost touching. But all Seren can do is stay in the same spot. She is paralysed by a mix of fear, and, surprising herself, excitement. Not many people get to see a polar bear up close like this. Seren realises that this bear, when it stands on all fours like it is now, it's actually not as tall as her. It's just a cub.

The cub's face looks at her curiously. Its face is all white apart from its black eyes and black nose. Seren thinks the cub looks a bit like Bili, he's also white with black eyes and black nose. Thinking of her cute, loving dog Bili makes her feel at ease with this creature in front of her, and without realising what she doing she moves up her hand and puts it under the cub's nose. She knows you are supposed to do this with dogs; you let them smell you and hope that they can tell from your scent that you are kind and mean no harm. Then, hopefully, they let you pet them.

The cub looks up at Seren from beneath long white eyelashes. Seren senses that the cub's eyes hold many mysteries, somehow, they look sad and tired, but inquisitive at the same time. The cub's black nose wrinkles as it gives Seren's hand a little sniff, and Seren wonders if a polar bear can still smell your scent when you have thick waterproof gloves on that are two sizes too big.

The cub seems happy with Seren's smell and it sits onto its back legs calmly, while keeping its eyes still locked onto her. Even sat down the cub is shorter than Seren, so she kneels to be at its level. This is another tip she has learned from her mam, she imagines her saying "whenever you are talking to younger children Seren, or young polar bears, it's important that you come down to their level, so they don't feel intimidated by you towering over them."

With both her knees firmly on the snowy ground Seren reaches out her right hand to pat the polar bear cub on the head. The cub doesn't seem upset by this, just curious, so while keeping her hand planted softly on the cub's head, she says out loud. "Hello, my name is Seren, my name means 'Star' in Welsh. I am a ten-year-old human girl. I come from South Wales which is in the United Kingdom. How about you?"

Seren still isn't sure that her abilities work on anything other than dogs but given the peril of her situation she figures it is worth a try. She listens hard for anything coming through to her from the cub's mind.

Slowly, but surely, she can make out something coming through the connection, it's very faint, but she thinks can make out one word, 'Love'.

"Love?" Seren asks the cub. "Is your name Love?"

"No," replies the cub. Seren can sense the cub's words more strongly now. "My name is Lova. It's Norwegian for 'warrior'. I am two-year-old girl polar bear cub." There's a pause in the message coming through. "I am from a place called Kongsfjorden. I have lost my mamma bear, have you seen her?"

"Lova, that's such a cool name. Well, I'm so pleased to meet you Lova, and thank you for not eating me." Seren states this with relief as she smiles sympathetically at the young cub and moves closer to her. "Sorry to hear you lost your mamma bear. I haven't seen her. I haven't seen any other polar bear actually! You are the first one I have ever seen in my whole life. I've lost someone too: my dad. Maybe you've seen him? He has a bright yellow coat on, so normally you can't miss him, but I guess maybe in this blizzard you can!" Seren chuckles, doing her usual trick of trying to make a joke out of a bad situation, but at least she's not on her own anymore.

With cold winds still blowing the snow all around them, Seren moves her body closer into the side of the cub. Soon she can feel the warmth of cub heating her up. She cwtches in even closer and puts her hand back onto Lova's head.

Lova continues, "my mother was captured by two men in black coats with their faces covered. I tried to chase after them, but the heavy snow appeared so quickly I lost sight of them. We had been walking for a few days, she is teaching me how to hunt and find food. We don't normally leave Kongsfjorden, but lately there have been fewer seals for us to eat there. We try to eat birds and eggs when we can't find any seals. We even have to eat bushes and moss sometimes, which are disgusting, they don't taste very nice at all. My mamma said the reason why it's hard for us to find food is because is because it's getting hotter in Svalbard, and it's all the humans fault. She said the husky dogs and the humans in Longyearbyen they have lots of food. So me and mamma, she is called Urszula, we decided to come here, even though it's a very long walk. Do you know why the humans would want to kidnap her?"

Seren cwtches in a little closer to Lova. "I have no idea why they would kidnap your mamma, no. But perhaps the people who took her are the same people who kidnapped the aurora scientists. That's why I am out here. My dad and I, and some others, are trying to help find the kidnapped scientists. I saw them getting taken by men in balaclavas while on a video call with Dr Owen you see. We think they might have taken them to the coal mine. Maybe your mother is there too, Lova!"

Chapter 22

Deep underground Skurk is scolding his friend. This happens a lot. "You should be able to do this by now. You really are an Idiot." The pair are sitting next to each other in the room lined with computer screens. They each have their own laptop open in front of them.

"We just need to change this climate data so the climate scientists working at the University of Svalbard don't notice how bad it really is here. If you edit the climate data too much it will be unrealistic, and the scientists will become suspicious." He points to Idiot's screen, "For this one about the atmosphere, you need to edit the data about the amount of carbon dioxide, so it looks like there has been no change since they closed the mine. That will make people think that closing the mine hasn't improved the air pollution, and that burning the coal isn't something we need to stop doing. Then they might open the mine back up again, do you see?" Skurk says sternly while pointing to the column marked *carbon dioxide concentration* in the spreadsheet on Idiot's screen.

"Yeah, I am much better at mining coal than I am at this data editing stuff," replies Idiot as he looks away from his laptop and up at the screens on the wall which have complicated graphs on them titled *Svalbard Glacier Mass* and *Barents Sea Temperature*. He lets out a loud sigh.

"Well, that is definitely true, you are useless at this," Skurk states judgingly, he laughs at Idiot, who by now is looking very confused and overwhelmed. "Anyway, just hurry up," Skurk continues, "we need to get this edited data back into the radar computers before a new batch of climate scientists arrive tonight to start analysing it. Based on the schedule we stole last week, the aurora scientists should be using it until 6pm tonight and then the climate scientists arrive at 9pm, so we have a three-hour window." Skurk turns back to his laptop and starts to frantically change the values on his own spreadsheet, then while still typing he says to Idiot,

"What about the scientists we have here? What are we going to do with them?"

Idiot responds, while attempting to edit the spreadsheet in front of him, "I don't know, I still don't understand how they were there at the radar. The schedule said there was a six hour stretch when it wasn't being used by anyone." He pauses, "although, I did have a look on Google earlier and it says the Sun is at its maximum activity right now, so there is a lot more aurora happening at the moment. Perhaps some aurora scientists booked extra days on the radar at the last minute to try take some more aurora data," states Idiot.

Skurk thinks for a moment before replying. "I guess it's possible, all these scientists just look the same to me. I just hope the boss can keep the police off our backs until we decide what to do with them. We could just take them in the tank further up the valley and chuck them out somewhere; I don't think they would last long very long in the snow with just those fleeces on."

Idiot gulps and says nothing in response to Skurk. All is quiet in the office apart from the sound of their furious typing.

Chapter 23

"Shall we go to the coal mine Seren? I want to find my mamma." Lova asks down the connection.

"Yes, we will go to the mine, of course. But for now, I think we should stay right here, we need to wait for my dad to find us. The snow seems to be falling less so hopefully he will be able to find us soon. You look in that direction," Seren points, "and I'll look this way. Look out for a man in a bright yellow coat," Seren replies, pointing to the opposite horizon.

The young pair stay huddled, cwtched together. Seren giggles and says proudly, "We look just like two Emperor Penguins Lova." Then she realises Lova probably doesn't know what an emperor penguin is, given they live on the opposite end of the world, in Antarctica!

Unbeknownst to Lova and Seren, only 300 meters away from them, Seren's dad is really starting to panic. Garry's been shouting Seren's name constantly ever since she went missing, but his shouts just keep getting carried away on the wind. After pacing a lot in many different directions and still not seeing Seren's purple coat and yellow hat, he turns to Dr Shaw and Juliet in despair. "I don't see how she could have got so far away from us in such a short space of time. Why can't we find her?" He looks like he might cry.

"Garry, your daughter is a smart girl, I am sure she has found somewhere safe to wait out the bad weather. It looks like it's clearing up slightly." After a pause Dr Shaw adds reassuringly, "Don't dismay, we will find her."

Finally, the swirly snow, that was making all the sky a pale white, lessens, and the wind stops its howling.

~~~

"I think the precipitation is stopping!" shouts Seren as she squints into the distance, "actually, I think I can see the arctic willow bush where I was trying to have a wee. Look Lova!"

In all the drama of losing her coat, getting lost, and making friends with a polar bear cub, Seren had totally forgotten about her desperate need to go for a wee. Somehow, she doesn't even need to go now!

Seren starts to scan the horizon near the arctic willow wee bush. Something yellow is moving back and forth. "Lova, I remember reading that polar bears have very good eyesight and can see long distances. Can you look over there by that bush and tell me if that moving yellow thing is a human?"

Lova gets up from the floor and plods in the direction of the arctic willow. Seren catches up and stands alongside her, she touches the cubs head and feels the answer from Lova: "Yes, that is a big human with a yellow coat. They have a black hat on, and they look stressed."

"Woah, you really do have good eyesight don't you, Lova." Seren announces, looking at her new friend in awe.

"That sounds like my dad. He is often stressed, but I think losing me will make him even more stressed than usual. Ok, I think we are probably alright to move from this spot now that we can see him. Let's start walking that way and I'll shout out to him."

~ ~ ~

"Can you hear something?" Juliet asks Dr Shaw.

"Yes, it sounds like someone shouting 'Dad'!" says Dr Shaw smiling. She dashes to catch up with Garry's frantic pacing.

"Garry, we can hear Seren. She's calling out to you!"

Garry spins around and starts to scan the horizon. "What! I can't hear anything?"

Dr Shaw, of course, isn't aware that all Seren's Dad's loud TV watching has made him mildly deaf, so it makes sense that he wasn't the first to hear his daughter's shouts.

"I see her!" he exclaims, running toward the purple figure. As he gets close to Seren, his joy turns to fear as he realises that walking next to his daughter is a real-life polar bear.

Chapter 24

"Seren!" Garry shouts, "Get away from that polar bear! Oh my gosh! Dr Shaw do you have the flares? Quick!" his head whips around in panic, he starts running toward his daughter.

Seren replies as he gets closer. "Oh Dad, don't be so silly. This is Lova, she is my friend. We think her mamma, Urszula, I hope I pronounced that right Lova? Is at the coal mine too. She was also kidnapped by men in balaclavas, not too far from here."

Seren's Dad stands in the snow, speechless.

Only his daughter could get lost for 15 minutes and manage to make friends with a polar bear in that time. As Dr Shaw and Juliet approach and step in line with Seren's Dad, they are also rendered speechless by the scene before them. Seren stands calmly, smiling back at her dad, she then turns to Lova and strokes the tufts of white fur on the top of her head, just like she does with Bili.

Before anyone has chance to ask any further questions, the sky above them lights up in dancing swirls of green. As everyone looks up towards the lights, the illuminations jiggle about more furiously and brighten up more and more of the dark sky with many different shades of green.

Seren, not usually lost for words, can't think of anything to say that can do justice to the amazing scenes unfolding in the sky above her. Instead of commentating on everything happening, she just arches her head back and intensely stares upwards, afraid to blink in case as she misses it.

The spectacular show continues above with curtains of red darting down to join the green below. Seren's mouth falls open further as the lights get brighter and brighter.

Garry is the one to ruin the quiet of this magical moment that everyone is having.

"Woah! That's the Northern Lights then?"

"It sure is," answers Juliet in a whisper, smiling up at the mystical sky and taking in a breath. "I have seen it more than ten times since I started my science research on the aurora, but every time I see it, it's a totally different experience. It moves different, it makes different shapes, the brightness of the colours, the red, green and pink is different. We want to understand about all these things the aurora does; it's shape, movement and fuzziness, for our science. That's what the 'Aurora Zoo' project is all about, and collecting data on this is what I do for my PhD. But just standing underneath it, enjoying this show that nature is putting on for us, being able to witness it with my own eyes; it is just so magical, it's so hard to put into words."

"I agree," Dr Shaw adds whimsically, "I've probably seen it more than fifty times now. I am just so lucky that this," she arches back further, "this is my job." She opens her hands to the sky as if she's presenting a slide show to the group. Her smile is so big it bends all the way up to her eyes, but none of the others see her massive smile, they are all looking up at the lights.

Silence descends on the group again, a silence inspired by the increased brightening of the aurora dancing into a new part of the sky. Dr Shaw sighs with happiness.

"This view, it truly never gets old."
"So why is it all those different colours?" asks Garry, still looking up in awe.

"Well," answers Dr Shaw, "every element in the air emits light of a different colour when it gains energy. The particles from the Sun have lots of energy and, when they reach the air in the atmosphere, they excite the different elements. They transfer their energy to the oxygen and nitrogen and that causes those gases to glow. The oxygen is responsible for the red and green aurora and the pinky-purple light, which is usually lower down than the green, is from the nitrogen."

Seren, meanwhile, is still uncharacteristically quiet, but of course she already knows about the colours.

Her dad asks her directly, "Seren, what do you think of your first aurora then? I hope this makes up for not seeing it in Wales?"

His words seem to knock her out of her hypnotic state slightly, at least enough for Seren to turn her body toward her dad. She keeps her eyes locked in their upward gaze towards the red and green lights that still frolic about above her though.

After a bit of a delay and with much enthusiasm, Seren finally screams out her answer to her dad, "I think it's just absolutely AMAZING!"

Still not taking her eyes off the sky Seren excitedly stamps her boots one by one, making deep imprints in the snow. She moves her arms out to her sides as if she's a bird of prey with its wings outstretched. She soars.

Then as the aurora movement above her changes timing, she matches it by moving her arms up and down. It's almost like she's become a flying aurora arc.

"Oh my gosh, I can see some pink! I really can't believe this is happening!" she screeches. She starts spinning around with her arms still out at her side. All the time she is looking up. The aurora changes brightness again and Seren starts to stamp her feet, moving them in time with the green, red and pink lights above. They move faster, so she stamps faster. "This is so epic!" she screams at the top of her lungs. She only stops spinning and stamping when she bumps into the side of Lova and almost falls onto her back.

"Oops, I am sorry, Lova!" Seren says dizzily to her friend as she pats down the white fur on her back. She reaches her hand across to Lova's head. "What do you think of the aurora, Lova?" she says aloud and waits.

"Do you mean those green lights in the sky, Seren? Mamma calls them the 'Nordlys'. She says that they are spirits in the sky on their way to the afterlife. I quite like that idea. Although another polar bear cub I grew up with, he said are an omen from the gods, and they mean something bad is about to happen, like bad weather or an upcoming battle."

Chapter 25

In their cramped cell Dr Dan turns to his PhD student, "Charlie, I overheard them talking in the corridor just now. It seems like they are editing weather data, and one of them isn't doing it right."

"That's curious," replies Charlie. "I wonder why they are editing weather data. Do you think it could be to do with why they kidnapped us? They do seem to think we are climate scientists." Charlie hugs his blanket to himself and tries to stop shivering.

The group, Dr Owen, Dr Dan, Charlie and Austen have all been struggling with the cold inside their bare cell. All of them are just wearing the grey fleeces they had on when they were kidnapped, none of them have a coat. The kidnappers have given them each a blanket, but they are not very thick. Even Austen, who was born in Norway and has lived in Svalbard for over ten years cannot deny that it really is very, very cold. He keeps fantasizing about chipping the coal off the walls and burning it to make a fire right there in the middle of the cell floor, but with nothing to light it, this dream is impossible.

Dr Owen, normally so chatty and energetic, is sitting on the bare floor, quiet and withdrawn. She started off their time in captivity as the most positive person in the group. She was the one saying over and over that help would come, but today her mood has dropped. She has spent most of her day asleep on the floor, curled up into a ball. She only woke to eat the small portions of food they were brought earlier. While she slept Dr Dan and Charlie agreed they are very worried about her.

"Why do you think the polar bears are locked up over there, Austen?" asks Charlie trying to distract himself from his worries about Dr Owen and his empty stomach.

"I'm not sure to be honest," Austen responds thoughtfully. "None of this seems to make sense to me. We used to get a few polar bears coming into Longyearbyen each year, I assume because they were looking for food. The number of them coming in has been steadily rising; six last year and three the year before that. But recently, the last six months of so, we haven't had any polar bears coming in. It's very surprising because the number of bears we encountered was growing, but now it's suddenly dropped off to none. My only idea is that those three polar bears over there were on their way into Longyearbyen and the bad guys kidnapped them too. But why kidnap polar bears?" asks Austen.

Dr Dan looks over at the skinny bears. They are all malnourished and in a much worse state than the four of them. "Well, the kidnappers aren't spending much money on feeding them, they look so hungry," Dan says, feeling genuinely sorry for the bears. "They do have strict rules on the killing and hunting of polar bears here in Svalbard, so maybe they didn't kill them because they are scared of being sent to prison. But, they have kidnapped us, so they can't be that worried about prison, can they? They must be keeping them alive for some reason, but I have no idea what that could be."

"I think it must be something to do with money," says Charlie. "Most crimes can be traced back to money. I know this cos I watch a lot of crime dramas. I just don't know how you would make money off three live polar bears," he says, hugging the blanket to himself. Before Dr Dan can respond with another theory, they hear footsteps coming down the corridor and the voice of a woman who seems rather angry.

"I've not heard this voice before," Dr Dan whispers to Austen and Charlie. "Whoever she is, it sounds like she's the one in charge!"

Chapter 26

"What on earth were you guys thinking? Kidnapping the scientists from the radar station! Why did you do that? I know this one is an idiot, but I thought you had more sense, Skurk!" shouts the boss before slamming the door to the office behind her.

Skurk looks up from his keyboard in shock at the sudden arrival of his boss in the room. "We weren't expecting anyone to be at the radar!" he says, while Idiot keeps his head down looking at his keyboard, speechless.

The boss sits on the spare seat beside them and her anger and aggression is replaced with despair. Her shoulders slope down, and she puts her head in her hands, her thick ginger hair falling across her face. Then after letting out a big sigh, she brings her head up and looks Skurk in the eye. "I can't believe our only chance at getting the mine back open and showing the people of Svalbard that climate change isn't as bad as everyone thinks it is, is down to you two fools. It's all such a mess!" She puts her head back in her hands, then after a short silence she asks, "have you at least finished editing the climate data?"

Skurk replies, doing his best to sound confident and able. "We've almost finished, Boss. Another thirty minutes, and we'll be done and then we can take the USB stick with the edited data on back down the mountain. We will make sure we are down before 9pm, before the climate scientists arrive."

"I wish we had someone who could just hack into their system, it would be so much easier to do this over the internet rather than having you two going back and forth in a stolen tank with a USB stick." She laughs to herself and then gives both Idiot and Skurk a very ungenuine smile. "I guess not many coal miners have side hustles as computer hackers; there's probably no need for it." She laughs again, Skurk and Idiot are too afraid to laugh with her.

"What about those polar bears? Have you heard from your friend in America who wanted to buy them for his circus, Idiot?" says the boss. Before

Idiot can answer her question, she continues. "It was a good idea you had, Skurk, to stop the polar bears heading into Longyearbyen. Now there are none turning up in town, the residents might start to think everything is fine with the glaciers and the climate of Svalbard. I am starting to hear more of the local people talking about a climate hoax. That's good news for us." She pauses and looks at her two employees, but they are both still too nervous to join the conversation. "Although, I don't really want to waste our money feeding the three of them. Idiot, get onto your showman friend in America, ok? We need them gone."

Idiot finally looks up from his keyboard. "Will do, Boss," he answers weakly.

Skurk changes the subject, asking with genuine concern, "How is your dad doing, Boss?" The boss's dad was good friends with Skurk and Idiot when they worked down the mine together, in fact they saw him as a father figure. There are hundreds of miners in Norway in the same position as Skurk, Idiot and the boss's dad. Many of them struggle to adjust to new lives, mining is all they have ever known. Most of them do not kidnap scientists or try to intercept and falsify climate data in a foolish effort to get the coal mine back open though.

Nevertheless, this was the only plan the boss could think of to help her dad and the other miners. She, Skurk and Idiot were convinced that their plan was guaranteed to work. They would trick the Government into thinking that the burning of the coal from the mine wasn't affecting Svalbard's climate. Then they would open the mine back up and give the miners back their jobs.

Simple.

Chapter 27

Seren's purple coat is making her highly visible against the white snow at the front of the group as Lova walks along next to her. "Dr Shaw is that the coal mine?" asks Seren, pointing into the distance.

There, atop a grey rocky incline stands three dark cylindrical towers. Each tower has a metal shoot that slants from the tower down to the snowy ground. They each stand much taller than Seren's house.

Dr Shaw answers, "Yes Seren, that's Mine 7. This was the last mine that closed. It is quite sad to think that once this place would have been bustling with activity: miners, trucks of coal, mine shafts going up and down, and now it is all silent."

Or is it?

Suddenly Seren notices a large vehicle moving away from the coal mine, its wheels struggling with the thick snow, even with the chains on. It makes slow progress into the distance. It's moving slowly enough for Seren to see the back number plate and recognise it. "That's Detective Dorritt's car!" shouts Seren, turning around to look at the others. Her sudden shouting makes Lova tense and dig her paws into the ground.

Seren's dad runs to catch up with her, "What did you say Seren? I didn't hear you."

"Oh, Dad you really need to get your hearing tested," Seren says, looking wearily at her father. "That was Detective Dorritt's car! She must have been in the mine!" she shouts urgently, looking from her dad to the others.

By now, Dr Shaw and Juliet have caught up too. "Why would Detective Dorritt be at the mine?" Dr Shaw asks. "Do you think maybe the police figured it all out and she's just rescued everyone?"

"She must have gone down to the police station to get the snow chains for her wheels. Maybe while she was there, they got a new lead? But why hasn't she called us to tell us her suspicions? If she thinks our friends are in the mine, we should know. She knows we are looking for them; it's all a bit suspicious," says Seren seriously.

Seren starts to walk towards the mine with purpose, crunching her crampons into the snow with a fury. She turns back to the group who lag behind her. "Well, come on everyone! We have come this far, and I do not trust Detective Dorritt for one minute. My mam would definitely say 'she's a bit shifty!', so I think we need to go into the mine and see for ourselves what is going on!"

Lova rises her head up to new friend in agreement, but the rest of the group do not look so sure. Before they can decide on what they should do they hear a noise coming from the Mine 7 elevator shaft. It's moving. Someone is coming up in the lift.

"Quick, we need to hide!" Dr Shaw whispers, urgently.
"What about that big box thing with the white plastic cover over there," suggests Garry, pointing to

the left of one of the big towers. The group run and stand behind it so they can't be seen by whomever comes out of the shaft door. Juliet leans back against the white sheet and fiddles with it, nervously. Pulling at a hole in the sheet, she reveals part of the University of Svalbard logo. "Oh my gosh!" she whispers to Garry, leaning next to him, "I think this is the stolen tank from the observatory. Look!" Juliet lifts the sheet up to expose the thick tank tracks resting in the snow.

As Garry's about to respond, he notices Lova is not very well hidden, anyone coming out of the lift door will be able to see her easily. "Lova," he whispers, "you need to move in closer to the white sheet! Quick!"

But it is too late.

The lift door opens and Skurk and Idiot are looking right at the tank. "There's a polar bear!" shouts Skurk, still standing in the lift doorway. "Quick, Idiot, throw your knife at it." Skurk knows that Idiot is quite skilled when it comes to throwing his pen knife. When Idiot is bored, he entertains himself by repeatedly throwing his knife at the same spot on their living room wall. He's totally wrecked that wall, but at least, because of his skill, the damage is mainly just in one spot.

Flicking the knife out in one graceful movement, Idiot hurls it at the polar bear's behind. It stabs into Lova's pelt, right on her bum, next to her tail. She yelps in agony and the pitiful sound echoes off the high mountains around them.

Seren is about to scream out in response to her friend's distress, but luckily her dad predicts his daughter's reaction. He slams his hand over her mouth before any sound is released, pulling her back towards him at the same time.

Her dad doesn't want the bad men to find out they are there; right now, they only know about Lova.

Chapter 28

Even though Lova is in a lot of pain, and her wound means she can no longer stand up, she's made sure that she falls onto the snow in the direction of the men. She has done her very best to draw the bad men's attention away from her new friends.

"It's just a little cub," says Skurk, kicking Lova in the side as she lays on the ground with the penknife still in her. "Let's just stick this one in with the other polar bears and then we can get going down the mountain to the radar."

"How will we move it?" asks Idiot, looking from Skurk to the cub as he removes the penknife from Lova's bum. With the removal of the knife, her bleeding increases, and she yelps. Seren starts to shake with anger, the colour of the cub's blood looks so vivid and scary against the whiteness of the snow.

Skurk and Idiot each grab one of Lova's front paws and drag the poor cub into the lift shaft. The doors close behind them. All that is left to show they were there is an eerie red carpet on the snow, leading right up to the shaft door.

Seren wrestles her dad's hand from her face and then grabs hold of it. She starts trying to drag him toward the mine. "Dad! Come on!" She pulls on his arm, but he's stronger than her and he stays put. "We need to go after them right now!" Seren shrieks at him, her eyes wild. She wants to cry but she knows that will not help Lova.

"Ok, Seren. Calm down. Don't worry. We will get Lova back." Her dad says reassuringly, he cwtches his daughter and then crouches down next to her in the snow and looks into her eyes seriously. "We just need to wait a few minutes before we call the lift back up to the surface. If we do it straight after it's gone down, and the bad men have only just got out, they might hear it moving and wonder why it's going back up. We won't leave it too long; just long enough so they will have pulled Lova into the mine, away from the shaft door. We just need to wait a little."

Chapter 29

As the group descend into the mine, all squashed into the lift, Seren tries to focus on the bobble on Juliet's green bobble hat and not on Lova's blood all over the lift floor.

She thinks about that time her mam tried to teach her and India how to make their own bobbles out of wool. Seren forgot to tie the string around the middle of it, and just ended up with lots of short pieces of wool all over her bedroom floor. It was so funny! She thinks about telling the others the bobble story, but maybe this is one of those stories where people say, 'I guess you had to be there!'

The lift door opens, and a long dark corridor is revealed in front of them. All the walls and floors of the corridor are made of coal, with the ceiling and side wall reinforced with wooden beams. Juliet whispers to the group, "I read that Mine 7 is four-hundred meters below the surface. It's eerie, isn't it?"

"Yes, I've never been this deep underground," whispers Seren in reply. Every so often, as they walk, they are illuminated by powerful lights strapped to the wooden beams. The lights make the coal around them glisten as they walk past, and Seren is reminded of the last school disco she went to, it was the first time she had seen a disco ball in real life, and she really liked the way it made the floor and the walls light up. She wore a purple sparkly top and bought £1.50 worth of pick and mix and drank two cans of orange pop, which was a bit naughty because her mam said she was only allowed one can. As she walks, reminiscing about the school disco, she reaches a part of the long corridor where the lights are broken. Now the coal isn't sparkling, and it seems much more sinister. Looking all around at the walls of dark coal she wonders how long it would take to burn it all.

Seren's busy brain is helping to distract her from the sinister trail of Lova's blood along the ground ahead of them. The route the kidnappers must have taken with Lova, is obvious, though: there is only one possible direction out of the lift along the long corridor.

By the time they have walked for another four minutes down the corridor of coal, Seren's thoughts have moved on from the school disco back to the bad men. She's already imagined three different ways they could have hurt Lova. She really dislikes her busy brain, and her vivid imagination sometimes.

Unexpectedly the silence in the mine corridor is totally extinguished by an earth-shattering roar.

Seren jumps back against the wall. She whispers to her dad with certainty.

"That does not sound like Lova!"

Chapter 30

Lova's mamma bear, Urszula, hurls herself at the bars of her cell. Her large white body moves with such brute force that the cell bars rattle against the bolts that hold the bars to the mine wall. Shards of coal, once securely part of the wall, start to break out onto the floor as the bars become loose.

Urszula is starved and has lost over 15kg since being in this cell of coal and steel but seeing her cub bleeding and pulled along the floor by her front legs has stirred an anger inside her that she cannot contain. She stands up on her hind legs and grabs at the bars with her powerful front paws, holding her head up high as she finds a strength from deep within her.

A mother's love is a strong thing.

She roars again.

Lova has been dropped on the ground about two metres from the door of her mother's cell. Skurk and Idiot retreat against the walls. They are not used to seeing any of the polar bears looking so lively, and a fully grown polar bear standing on her hind legs roaring ever so loudly at them has come as quite a shock.

Seeing that her cub is still not fully conscious, even with all the lour roaring, Urszula grabs at the cell bars in a fury. Her claws curl around them. Her roaring seems to have inspired some action in her cell mates too and she is soon flanked with a polar bear each side of her. They start to match her timing, pushing on the bars below her paws with their heads.

Dr Dan, Austen, Dr Owen, and Charlie can do nothing but look on from their own cell in wonder at the love and chaos happening before them.

"Do something you idiot!' says Skurk, trying to push Idiot across the large cavern towards Urszula's cell. He looks at the bars and is momentarily impressed by how they are moving back and forth so freely while still bolted to the wall. "What can I do?" Idiot shouts back in distress, his eyes wide with fear.

"Your knife!" screams Skurk eyeing Idiot's pocket. Idiot fiddles with the penknife, trying to flick out the blade, but he can't get a good grip and starts to panic more as the sound of the cell bars rattling out of the walls gets louder. "Just let me do it!" Skurk yells, grabbing the penknife from his friend and walking towards Urszula. He holds the knife in his outstretched hand, like he's in a fencing competition.

The polar bear he's trying to battle with is twice his size, both width-ways and length-ways. Dr Owen stares at him thinking how scary it must be to be walking toward this wild animal, who is so incredibly large and suddenly so incredibly alive. She's thinks about how afraid Skurk looks, as he moves closer to the Urszula, who is still roaring loudly for her injured cub. As Urszula throws her large body against the bars again and one of the bolts come loose Idiot turns around and runs away down the corridor, abandoning his friend to the wrath of the mamma bear.

Chapter 31

"Dr Owen! We found you!" calls Seren as she and her dad enter the chaos of the cavern.

Dr Owen turns weakly to the young girl, "Oh my gosh Seren, what are you doing here?" she says. Her voice is husky and quiet, and she's so weak, but still, she gets to her feet by holding onto the cell bars and puts her tired face in-between them. She squints across the cavern in disbelief as this brave young girl, her dad and her two colleagues walk toward her. It's truly unbelievable that they could be here. The sight seems to make Dr Owen come alive; even smiling as she reminds Seren, "and I told you on our call, Seren, please just call me Julie!"

As much as Dr Owen and Seren want to continue their lovely conversation, they are interrupted by another loud roar from Urszula, which echoes around the cavern. The sheer scale of the sound coming from the large polar bear reminds Seren of the immediate task at hand: she has to save Lova.

As Seren turns towards the roaring bear, it's clear to her that the animal in most danger right now is not Lova, but Urszula, because Skurk is getting closer to her with the knife. "Juliet! He's going to stab Lova's mam! Stop him!" she screams.

Luckily Juliet is a very keen rugby player, so without even thinking, she rugby tackles Skurk to the ground and wrestles the penknife out of his hand, after she does this, she manages to get onto Skurk's back. She holds him firmly to the ground with all her might. Juliet throws the knife into the corner of the cavern, out of Skurk's reach, and continues to push her body down onto Skurk's spine so he can't move. Skurk's shouts are muffled as he wriggles under her and tries to get free. "Ger off me, you stupid woman!" he yells.

With Lova's mother safe from being stabbed, Seren and her dad quickly go to Lova's side and Seren starts to shake her gently. Lova seems to be very sleepy from the loss of blood. "Lova, I hope you don't mind but I am going to put my hand on your bum. I need to put pressure on your wound. I learned all about it in my first aid class; we need to stop the bleeding. I know your bum is your private part and normally I wouldn't touch you without your permission, but this is an emergency, and you are losing a lot of blood. Also, since you are a polar bear and don't wear clothes, you probably aren't so bothered about having your bum on show, like us humans are!" says Seren quickly, trying to remember her first aid training. She calmly presses one hand, then the other firmly onto the wound. Seren feels very grateful in this moment, because her ADHD means she is actually rather useful when other people are in a crisis.

While Seren is sat putting pressure on Lova's wound with both her tiny hands atop each other, Dr Shaw and Seren's dad help Urszula and the other polar bears with the cell bars. Dr Shaw and Garry pull on the bars from the outside in time with the polar bears pushing outwards from within the cell. With an almighty crack, one of the bars comes away from the wall and large coal chunks clunk off onto the floor below.

"It's working!" exclaims Seren's Dad. The bears look up and seem to understand what they must do next. They move closer to the wall, where the other bar is almost free. Dr Shaw and Garry both step back and go to shelter Seren and Lova from any debris that might come falling from the brittle walls.

Finding inspiration from Urszula's passion to help her wounded cub, the other polar bears work together to give one almighty push for freedom. The cell bars come completely out of the wall and crash down to the floor, blasting out more chunks of coal that bounce in all directions.

Black dust fills the cavern, and everyone stands still in shock.

The polar bears are free.

Chapter 32

Urszula bounds straight over to her wounded cub. She gives Lova's forehead a soft nudge with her black nose. Lova stirs, and slowly opens her eyes. The overwhelming love and relief from both bears is clear to everyone, and Lova seems to smile up at her mamma bear.

Seren did let go of Lova's wound on seeing this very large polar bear come running towards her. She jumped backwards next to her dad for safety, but now she sees that Urszula is calmer, and that Lova is still bleeding, she is eager to continue administering first aid to her new friend. She counts to nine in her head, deems that enough time for them to have a 'mother-daughter moment' and steps back towards them.

"Seren, what are you doing? Stay back!" shouts her dad, concerned to see his daughter walking towards a polar bear who was only seconds ago acting like an angry, scary beast.

Meanwhile, on the other side of the cavern, Skurk is still wriggling underneath Juliet. "Ger off me!" says Skurk, his face half squashed into the hard ground.

"Where are the keys for the other cell?" demands Juliet, "tell us where they are, and I might not tell the police that you tried to stab a polar bear; a protected species!"

"No! I'm not telling you," Skurk says looking shifty as his eyes dart toward the room down the corridor.

Dr Shaw, who is standing next to the mound that is Juliet on Skurk, notices his shifty look. "He just looked down the corridor. Maybe that's where the keys are. Sometimes your eyes give you away when you are trying to not tell the truth. There's a room down there, I'll run down and have a look, see if I can find them."

While Dr Shaw runs out of the cavern, Seren is back next to Lova pushing down on her wound, with her dad at her side.

"I'm so sorry that the bad men locked you and the other polar bears up, Urszula," Seren says. And I am so sorry we couldn't stop them hurting Lova." Seren is looking down at the cub, who seems to be waking up.

"If we can get Lova out of the mine to the tank then we should be able to get her down to Longyearbyen to get her some help." Seren looks at her dad, then over at Skurk. "I hope the bad guy who ran past us in the corridor hasn't taken the tank."

"That idiot can't drive the tank!" shouts Skurk bitterly. "It was always me who had to drive it. He just sat in the back with his ear plugs in the whole time because he gets too overwhelmed by the noise. He's so sensitive. He's probably up there somewhere crying in the snow right now."

Seren turns to him sternly, "You are a bad man, and I know that he is a bad man too, but my mam says that you shouldn't make fun of people who are sensitive. If people cry when they are upset, or get overwhelmed by loud noises, then that is totally ok!"

"Whatever!" grunts Skurk under his breath as Dr Shaw enters the room with a bundle of keys.

"I found them!" she says smiling. "They were in the top desk drawer; it wasn't even locked." She strides towards Dr Dan, Dr Owen, Charlie and Austen who are now all standing, clutching the bars of their cell. They look at Dr Shaw hopefully.

"I bet you are glad that you employed me to come work on the Aurora Zoo project with you Dan," states Dr Shaw, smiling at her boss. She starts working through the bundle of keys in her hand, pushing one key, then another, into the thick metal lock below Dan's hand. They hear a click.

"I sure am!" answers Dr Dan, smiling back at her, as the cell door swings open.

Chapter 33

Now that the scientists and the polar bear are all free, and the fighting is over, everyone gathers in the cavern around Lova and Seren.

Even Juliet and Skurk are now upright. After unlocking the cell, Dr Shaw found some rope on the ground and used it to tie Skurk's hands behind his back. Juliet still holds firmly onto Skurk though, so he can't run away. She pulls the criminal toward the group. When Urszula sees him approach she lets out a low growl right into his face. Skurk looks down, totally defeated, and Juliet stands proudly behind him.

"In all this excitement, I totally forgot about needing a wee! Has anyone seen a toilet anywhere?" asks Seren looking around the cavern. Everyone laughs, and all the tension of the underground battle is gone.

"I think I saw one inside the room where I found the keys, with all the screens in, I'll show you on our way out Seren," says Dr Shaw, smiling down at the young girl.

With the help of the other polar bears, Urszula has managed to lift Lova onto her back. The other two bears walk slowly either side of Urszula and they lead everyone down the corridor.

"Seren, do you know what a group of polar bears is called?" asks Dr Shaw as she and Seren's dad walk her toward the office with the loo.

"No. What is it called?" says Seren inquisitively.

"It's called a celebration!"

Whilst Dr Shaw, Seren and her dad are in the office. Dr Dan, Austen, Charlie and Dr Owen walk slowly along the corridor behind the celebration.

"Austen do you think polar bears can press lift buttons?" asks Charlie.

"Normally I would say no, but after seeing how they managed to destroy those cell bars, pressing an 'up button' on a lift might not be a problem?" Austen chuckles.

At the back of the group, Juliet pushes Skurk along in front of her. She grasps tightly at the rope wrapped around the criminal's hands. "I just don't understand why you did all this." Juliet says to Skurk has she forces him forward.

"The Boss said it was a fool proof plan," Skurk replies. "She said what we were doing would mean the government would have to open the mine back up, and we would get our jobs back! It was supposed to be simple. But then the space scientists were at the radar; they weren't supposed to be there, and Idiot supposedly had this contact who wanted the polar bears for the circus in America." He looks down at the floor in shame. "It sounds ridiculous when you say it out loud!" His shoulders slump as he walks along slowly.

"Who is 'The Boss'?" asks Juliet. Skurk is silent, his face screwed up in anger as he continues to look down at his feet.

"Ah, no worries, I am sure the police will get it out of you!" says Juliet, continuing to press the defeated man forward.

"Hah!" Skurk laughs. His face has a sudden look of defiance, "She is the police!"

Chapter 34

By the time Seren, her dad and Dr Shaw have successfully ascended the full 400 meters of mine shaft up to surface, the other two polar bears have gone. Seren feels a bit disappointed because she never got to say 'thank you' to them. Sensing his daughter's disappointment at missing the bears departure her dad says, "Seren they must have been very hungry, and after all polar bears are solitary animals; they don't like travelling in packs. Now that they are free, they probably just want to be alone".

This new knowledge about polar bears being solitary makes Seren think of a boy in her class, Dylan. He prefers to play on his own and he seems perfectly happy doing that; he gets really stressed when there are too many children around him. Seren smiles to herself as she makes a mental note to tell Dylan that he has something in common with a polar bear.

Urszula and Lova are already in the back of the tank, sitting on the middle of the floor, Dr Owen is in the back too. It really is a rather big tank. Seren, her dad and Dr Shaw join Dr Owen on the seats along the walls, facing inwards towards the bears. Luckily Austen knows how to drive the tank, so he is sat in the front with Dr Dan, and Charlie. As everyone is trying their best to get comfortable in the hard seats, the mine shaft door opens again and Skurk is shoved out of the lift door into the snow by Juliet. They make their way to the tank.

Dr Owen looks around at the space in front of her, which is mostly filled with polar bear. "Oh my, Juliet I am not sure where you are going to fit!"

Seren is optimistically attempting to make more room by bunching up closer to her dad. As she starts to shove herself towards him, there is suddenly the sound of a loud siren coming toward them up the valley.

A big police car, like the one Detective Dorritt had, speeds up to them with its blue lights flashing. Detective Noah gets out of the car and rushes toward Skurk, not noticing the large group inside the University of Svalbard tank to the left of him.

"Skurk? What are you doing here?" the detective asks him. "We tracked Dorritt's police car here, we think she might be something to do with the kidnapped scientists!" says Noah, looking confused as Juliet steps out from behind Skurk, and he sees that Skurk's hands are tied with rope.

"What on earth is going on?" Detective Noah exclaims, looking very shocked as he notices the back of the tank contains some of the people he met earlier, and two polar bears.

Austen leans out the front window of the tank, he shouts, "Hey Noah!"

In the back of the tank Seren whispers to her dad, "how do they all know each other?"

Dr Shaw overhears and explains, "Of course Noah knows Austen and Austen knows Skurk, because everyone knows everyone in Longyearbyen, it's so small it's not even big enough to be called at town remember, it's a just a 'settlement." She chuckles.

Leaning further out of the driver-side window Austen goes on explaining to Noah, "I'll drive these lot down the mountain in the tank. If you take Skurk and Juliet to the police station, we will meet you there. You should arrest Skurk and put him in handcuffs, he was the one who kidnapped us all. It seems Detective Dorritt was his boss, and this whole thing was her idea!" he announces coolly, before firing up the tank's engine.

If there was any chance of Detective Noah gathering more information about the situation, it is completely destroyed by of the loud thrumming of the tank's engine.

No one can hear anything.

As the metal tank treads that go over the wheels start to move along the snowy ground, the tank seems to get even louder. Seren holds on tight to her dad as her small body starts to rattle in the metal seat, and Lova, sitting on top of her mamma appears to hold on tighter too.

Chapter 35

Detective Noah drives Juliet and Skurk down the
mountain very slowly in the thick snow, he's feeling
a bit lost for words. Finding out that your partner is
actually a criminal mastermind and that one of your
friends, Skurk, is in on it all is definitely a big
enough shock for one day. But then to see two polar
bears in the back of a tank; he thinks it's all a bit
much.

Juliet sits in the passenger seat beside the detective,
she switches from looking at the snow sticks ahead
of the car to eyeing the prisoner in the back. He still
has his head down, looking defeated. She turns back
to watch the snow sticks, the only thing that breaks
up the landscape ahead of them.

"Hey, look, there's someone in the snow!" Juliet
exclaims, pointing forwards.

As Noah brakes harshly to avoid hitting them,
Skurk's head smacks into the metal cage in the
police car that separates the front and back seats.

Detective Noah gets out of the car and walks slowly over to the person huddled in the snow. "Hallo!" he shouts, walking over to them. When he gets close enough, he puts his hand softly on their back, "Hallo, are you ok?"

Idiot looks up at Detective Noah. He has clearly been crying, his eyes are blood shot, his face is red, and he must be very cold because his lips look a lot more blue than pink.

"Oh, Lucas." Noah says putting his hand out to help his friend up, "I guess you were involved in Detective Dorritt's scheme too, huh?" he sighs.

Idiot doesn't answer, he just shivers, still huddled in the snow. After a few seconds of silent shivering, he decides to take the help being offered and grips the detective's hand. Noah pulls him up from the ground with an awkward smile. Idiot dusts himself down, still shaking. He walks toward the car, his spirit crushed.

As Noah opens the back door of the police car, Idiot sees his 'friend' Skurk looking back at him. Skurk has a big red mark on his forehead, and his hands are handcuffed in front of him, he gives Idiot a look of total disgust.

Before Idiot gets into the police car to sit next to Skurk, two criminals together with their failed plan, he turns back to look at Detective Noah.

"Thank you for calling me by my actual name, Noah. It means a lot. Everyone has called me Idiot for so long, you know, I almost forgot that my actual name is Lucas!"

Chapter 36

For Seren, the novelty of travelling in the back of a borrowed military tank wore off after a total of three minutes. The tank was so loud, with everything rumbling and vibrating, and all she could do was grip her dad's leg and hold on tight, while he covered both her ears with his hands to try to muffle the over-powering sound. Seren has decided that 'a tank' has now moved up to the number one spot on her 'most disliked sounds' list. It's closely followed by hand dryers and hoovers.

When the tank finally arrived in Longyearbyen, the police and the government vet had already been waiting there for fifteen minutes. Detective Noah had radioed ahead to tell them what was needed.

Austen is first out of the tank. As he walks around to the back to let the rest of the group out, he's knocked down into the snow by a furry grey mass.

"Milo!" shouts Austen. "It's so nice to see you boy!" The old husky dog does his usual excited howling with his nose into the sky, and then jumps up at Austen's cheeks and nose. Milo licks Austen's face furiously.

Luckily for the people still waiting to be let out the back of the tank, Charlie has the sense to walk past the lovely scene of Milo and Austen being reunited and opens the back door of the tank to set them all free.

Urszula jumps down first with Lova still securely on her back. The cub looks distressed, and her mamma's once white back is now dark red with her cub's blood. The vet approaches mother and cub carefully as the rest of the group clamber down from the tank and stand beside them.

"Hallo, my name is Dr Amy Hansen. I am the local vet." Dr Amy stares at the two polar bears in front of her. Looking at Urszula's massive body, she realises that she's never actually been this close to a full-sized, fully conscious polar bear. When she has seen them in the wild, they have been sleeping, or if she's doing a treatment on them, they are always tranquilized. Amy looks nervous but takes a deep breath inwards and that seems to calm her. "It is going to be difficult to transport your cub to my surgery, but I should be able to clean their wound right now. Then I'll stitch it all up and give them some antibiotics. I can do all that out here."

Amy realises she is talking to a polar bear.

Seren walks alongside her and before Dr Amy can even attempt to stop her the young girl she rests her hand on the cub's head. It's strange because the girl doesn't say anything out loud to the cub, but it clear that she is also 'talking' with a polar bear.

"It's going to be ok, Lova," says Seren in her mind, sending encouragement down the connection with Lova. "This nice vet, Dr Amy, she is going to help you. She has a purple bobble hat on, and a kind face, so I think we can trust her."

Chapter 37

At the Politistasjonen, Skurk and Lucas have been formally arrested for their crimes and put into separate cells. Detective Noah has been on the phone ever since he got back to the station, trying to do all he can to find his partner. His police colleagues were able to track Detective Dorritt to her father's street; her police car has built-in GPS, so they were able to find it quite quickly. But it seems she remembered about the GPS just in time and abandoned the police car there and then got away in a car that was parked nearby. Her criminal knowledge obviously extends to stealing cars.

The Norwegian police who welcomed the tank into Longyearbyen were quick to transport all the humans in the group to the police station, where they were all swiftly given a nice a cup of tea and a warm blanket. Seren picked the blue one to wrap around herself, it was the only one that wasn't grey (her least favourite colour).

The group were all interviewed individually, apart from Seren who was, of course, interviewed with her dad. The police were all very apologetic. It seems they had no idea that Detective Dorritt was the boss of a group editing climate change data in an ambitious attempt to reopen the last mine in Svalbard.

After the interviews were complete, and everyone had drunk at least two cups of tea, the whole group; Austen, Milo, Charlie, Dr Shaw, Dr Dan, Dr Owen, Seren and her dad reunite in the staff room with the blue comfy chairs. It seems like weeks since Seren was last in this room. So much has happened since she was here meeting Milo for the first time. It's hard for her to believe that it was only two days ago.

"Dad!" says Seren suddenly, staring wide-eyed at her dad. "We should ring Mam back in Wales and tell her we are ok! She must be worried sick!" Seren speaks quickly, falling over her words as her brain works faster than the mouth. She pats down her pockets and realises her phone isn't there. "I think I have lost my phone again Dad. That's annoying, can

I used yours to call her? Because I also need to tell her that I saw the northern lights and that I even saw a pink aurora, and it was amazing! And that I made friends with a polar bear cub called Lova and I helped rescue the scientists and Austen the engineer and talked with Milo the husky dog. Oh, and I met Lova's Mam, Urszula, mustn't forget that. And how we figured out that the bad guys were in the coal mine and now they are in jail, but they haven't caught Detective Dorritt yet, which is bad, but I'm sure they will. And I need to tell her I met a vet called Dr Amy who has a purple hat!"

Everyone smiles at this brave, surprising, young girl and her hilarious summary of this crazy adventure they've all been on. Dr Shaw thinks to herself that if she hadn't witnessed all of this with her own eyes then she would surely never believe this wild story.

It had all really happened.

Garry looks at his daughter with pride. He loves the way she sees the world, and her excitement about it all, despite the danger she was in. He swiftly removes his phone from his pocket to give it to her. Seren taps at the screen, but the phone is black; it's totally dead. "We will have to find a charger for it Seren or borrow the police phone. I guess phone batteries don't do well in the cold huh?" her dad chuckles. Seren doesn't go immediately to find a charger for the phone though. Instead, she tells the group about a YouTube video she watched all about how batteries work. They all listen in silence, fascinated by her knowledge, and the fact that she still has the energy to talk so enthusiastically about batteries.

Juliet left the staff room after only a few minutes of chatting with everyone. As soon as she knew the full story of all that happened, she felt incredibly restless. Noah has kindly allowed her to use one of the spare desks at the station to access her university email account. As a fellow scientist, she felt compelled to write an email right away to tell the climate scientists all that had happened. They need to know that all their climate data was being edited by Skurk and Lucas in their underground lair at the mine. If her aurora data was all wrong, she would need to know straight away. It's so important to her that the scientists know to go back through everything and remove all the fake data. Otherwise, all the climate models for Svalbard will be incorrect.

Chapter 38

After a very long conversation with her very worried Mam on the police station landline phone, Seren explains to her mam that she has to go now and say a final goodbye to Lova.

Detective Noah finishes his own phone calls and insists on giving Seren and Garry a lift back to the edge of the settlement of Longyearbyen, where Dr Amy has just finished stitching up Lova's wound.

When they arrive, Garry and Noah hang back and even Urszula moves away to let her cub have a moment with her human friend. Seren kneels next to Lova, she thinks that the cub looks one hundred times better than she did earlier in the cavern. Lova can't sit back on her bum because it will hurt her, so she lies on her side and Seren lies down on her side in the snow facing her. Seren once again puts her hand onto Lova's head fur. She does speak out loud but only in a whisper. She feels a bit shy about what she is going to say and doesn't want the others to hear, it's private.

"Lova, how are you feeling?" asks Seren. She doesn't wait for an answer, because she needs to get her own feelings out before she gets distracted, and her thoughts go off track.

"I told my mam all about you. She was very shocked to hear that I had made friends with a polar bear cub. I don't think she believed me to be honest." She pauses, smiling, but suddenly feeling very sad.

"Now, I know you must stay here in Svalbard, and I know that I have to go back to South Wales with my dad. But I really do wish you could come visit me sometime. It is pretty cold in Wales. I think you would be fine, honestly. You could meet my mam, and my best friend India. She would love you. Bili, my dog, he would love you too, we always say he looks like a little polar bear, because he's all white and fluffy too."

Seren takes a big breath because she is beginning to struggle with her emotions. "I know we have only known each other for like two days, but we've been through such a lot, and I am so glad I have met you. I am so glad I saw the aurora for the first time with you. I've been thinking about it, and I think the biggest part of the magic of seeing the northern lights is who you see it with." She pauses in this magical memory.

"It was so much more wonderful because I was there with you. I am so happy we had that moment together under the green, dancing light. I will never forget it, I promise."

Seren starts to feel like she might cry. Her body feels all hot, even though it is still minus twenty degrees. Seren just hates goodbyes so much. However, she shakes off her sadness because she is determined to finish telling her friend all that she set out to say.

"I hope that you and your mamma bear will be ok, and that you find some tasty food very soon. She definitely needs a good meal after what she has been through. When I get back to Wales Mam says I can have my Nan's Sunday dinner even though it won't be a Sunday, I am so excited for that because it's my favourite meal!" Seren pauses and licks her lips, imaging her Nan's delicious cooking. "I assume you have never tried gravy, but if you ever get the chance, Lova, you should. It's amazing. It even makes broccoli and carrots taste nice!"

It's quite a while before Lova's reply comes down the connection to Seren, and it seems weaker than before. Seren wonders if that is due to all the blood that Lova lost, but eventually a message gets through.

"Seren, I am so glad we met also. Thank you so much for helping me find my mamma bear and doing first aid on me. I think you saved my life. Whenever I see the aurora, I will think of you, and I will remember this time we had together. I always thought that all humans were bad, because my mamma told me how it is their fault that the glaciers are melting and that's the reason there aren't so many seals for us to eat. Now that I have met you and made friends with you, I have hope for the future. I know that not all humans are bad. Seren, you are so brave and caring. You must never change because you are so awesome just the way you are. I am very jealous that Bili dog gets to spend so much time with you!"

Seren thinks Lova's message has finished, but then there is a whisper of something else. "Sometimes when we struggle to find food, my mother tries to make me eat moss off the rocks. It's so disgusting! I wonder if gravy would make moss taste better. What do you think?"

"I think it definitely would, Lova" says Seren, laughing out loud. She stands up slowly, and Lova turns over, gets up onto her four legs and gives her friend a final nod. Urszula moves alongside Lova, and Garry comes and stands next to Seren.

"Well, I hate goodbyes, Lova, so I won't say goodbye. This is just a 'see you soon'," Seren gives Lova's head fur one last rub, and the bears plod away from them.

Seren waves enthusiastically at the bears, even though both of them, mamma and cub, have their backs to her as they walk into the distance. They get so far away that their outlines start to blend in with the snow making them hard to see.

Just when Seren was about to stop waving because she felt a bit silly, Lova turns her head back to get one last look at her new friend.

Seren shouts after her.

"Don't forget to think of me when you see the aurora, Lova!"

Chapter 39

Juliet hauls her large suitcase across Svalbard airport toward the check-in desk for Norwegian Air. She looks around for everyone else and sees Seren's yellow hat and purple coat. The group are all sitting in the corner, waiting for her.

"Seren, the Governor of Svalbard is outside," says Juliet, pulling her case towards the group. "She wants to thank you for all you have done before you leave."

"Oh, the Governor? That sounds cool!" Seren shouts as she runs up to Juliet and looks past her at the sliding airport doors.

The Governor is not at all what Seren was expecting; she was thinking of a 'Town Mayor' type character, like they have in the UK. She imagined a cheery old woman with greying hair, a long flowery dress and a big gold chain around her neck. Instead, the woman was head to toe in bright green waterproof clothing, with big, heavy looking, camel-coloured boots, like you might see someone wearing on a building site. She also wears a mustard-coloured beanie hat and a thin scarf around her neck that is camouflage patterned.

"Hi Seren, my name is Anna-Kristin," announces the Governor, putting her hand out for Seren to shake. "I am the Governor of Svalbard, and we are so thankful to you and your dad and the other scientists. You really did save the day. Our climate scientists have asked me to thank you too. They are frantically trying to sort out all the climate models, so we have accurate data." She pauses, looking down at the young heroine.

"Anyway, I am just so glad I got to catch you before you fly back to the UK." The Governor smiles and then continues. "If it was possible, I would show you our thanks by giving you the 'key to the city', but since Longyearbyen is only a settlement, I can't do that because no key exists!" Anna-Kristin chuckles to herself, and although Seren doesn't really understand, she laughs with her, because it seems polite.

"But anyway, Seren, honestly," Anna goes on, crouching down to be level with Seren, "if you ever do want to come back to Svalbard, you are most welcome. I will make sure you and your family have a place to stay, free of charge, and we can organise all sorts of fun activities for you. There's lots of things to do here in Svalbard, like snowmobiling and husky sledding, whatever you like really!"

Seren is delighted. "Thank you so much Governor Anna-Kristin. I definitely want to come back. You are so lucky you live here!"

Chapter 39

Seren slept on all three flights back to Southampton. The only time she perked up was in the gift shop in Tromsø airport, when she became utterly determined to find a souvenir fridge magnet. Seren always buys a fridge magnet to remember the places that she has travelled to, and because of all the chaos that happened in Svalbard, she totally forgot about this very important souvenir. Although she is only ten years old, Seren thinks she is doing quite well, collecting magnets and places. She currently has four magnets in her collection: Tenerife, Bournemouth, Disney Land Paris and the Brecon Beacons. Some of her friends say the Brecon Beacons one shouldn't count, they say "it doesn't count as 'travelling' if you're born in Wales, live in Wales, and then go somewhere in Wales." Seren thinks they are wrong though, the Brecon Beacons counts because it is so epic, and her parents agree.

The magnet she buys to remember her fifth place travelled to; Norway, is her favourite magnet in her collection so far. It has a painting of a mother polar bear on it, with her little cub. There is also green and pink aurora above them, and lots of snow, and the word 'Norway' in capitals below the bears. Seren describes it to her dad as "super cute" and says that it reminds her of Lova and her mamma bear.

Back in the UK, Seren's mam, Stella, has been waiting patiently at Southampton airport for her husband and daughter to return. She's been in the arrivals area for almost two hours already. Stella always insists on getting to airports early, even if she isn't the one flying. Seren's nan and Bili have also come to welcome back the adventurers; but her Nan has to stay outside with Bili, since dogs aren't allowed into airports.

Seren, her dad, Dr Dan, Dr Owen, Dr Shaw, Juliet and Charlie all come out of arrivals together. As they walk side by side pulling their cases behind them, Seren jokes "look at us, we are like a 'Science Squad', all walking in line!"

When Seren sees her mam standing in arrivals, her fellow 'Science Squad' members are forgotten in an instant. She abandons her case in the middle of the arrivals floor, runs up to her mam and wraps her arms around her neck and her legs around her waist.

There's nothing quite like a cwtch with your mam.

"Mam, I have missed you so much!" she shouts into her mam's ear.

"I've missed you too Seren, but there is no need to shout." Seren releases her mam and smiles up at her excitedly. By the time Seren goes in for another cwtch, the 'Science Squad' have all caught up to them.

"You must be Mrs Jones," says Dr Owen, pushing her luggage along in front of her. "It's such a pleasure to finally meet you. You should be very proud of your daughter. I wouldn't have made it out alive from that mine if it wasn't for her determination and bravery."

Stella looks down at Seren, who is still holding her tightly. "I am always proud of my Seren, but thanks for reminding me just how amazing my little girl is."

Dr Owen announces to the group, "We'd happily put your family up in a hotel in Southampton tonight, so you don't have to rush back to Wales. There's an amazing science centre nearby in Winchester that Dr Dan and I could take you to tomorrow. I think Seren would love it, and it really would be our pleasure. They actually have a new planetarium show running right now all about the aurora, and they have a new workshop we designed about our research called 'Aurora Art', which is all about our Aurora Zoo project!" Dr Owen says enthusiastically.

"Oh Mam, that sounds amazing. Can we go?" asks Seren, pulling on her mother's arm. "Please say yes!"

"Ok Seren, we can stay. But I don't know what we are going to do with Bili. I assume dogs aren't allowed in science centres!" Stella chuckles.

"What!" Seren screams. "Bili is here?" Seren runs out of the door of the arrivals area looking quickly left and right.

Outside Seren sees her nan but before she can say hi to her, Bili jumps up on her wagging his long tail furiously. Then with his front paws on Seren's coat, and his tail still wagging he licks at his best friend's chin with great vigour.

"Bili, I got so much to tell you."

Chapter 40

Inside the Winchester planetarium, on one of the one-hundred-and-seventy-six reclining seats sits Seren. She rests her head back and stares up into the ceiling of the dome, "I am so excited," she whispers. Her mam is one side of and her nan on the other, they are both enjoying the comfy reclining seats too. Three generations of women all look up at the curved ceiling above them and smile with contentment and wonder as the colourful floor lights go out and small pin pricks of light, simulating stars, come into focus all around them.

A calming voice fills the dome. "Hello everyone, welcome to the Winchester Science Centre and Planetarium. My name is Cordi, and I am your planetarium presenter today. In this show, we will start by giving you a tour of the stars, the constellations, and the planets that you can see in the night sky tonight. I can fly us in for a closer look at the planets, and we can see some constellation art too. It's a live show, so it's totally up you where we go." Cordi pauses, watching the audience's faces in the dim light and turns up the brightness of the stars in the sky on her control panel. She always feels quite powerful in this bit of the show. Seren and her family are all arching back as far as their seats will allow to get the very best view; their mouths hanging open in awe.

"Look at all those stars Nan, aren't they pretty?" Seren whispers, her nan doesn't say anything in reply. Seren realises that her nan is totally speechless, hypnotised by this amazing simulation of the night sky above them. She had told Seren as they walked over to their reclining seats earlier, "even though I have lived over sixty years on this Earth, this is actually my first time in a planetarium Seren."

Cordi loads up the next part, "now I am showing you some high-definition footage of the aurora filmed in Norway. While we look at all the amazing shapes and movement of the aurora, I will talk you through how the aurora is formed, and what you might see if we have another solar storm in the UK, like the one that we had last week."

As the green swirls start their dance around the planetarium dome Seren says quietly to herself, "Hey Lova." She smiles up at the magical northern lights, and wonders what her polar bear friend is doing right now.

The green lights that curl far and wide are suddenly joined by red stripes of light, they seem to reach right into deep space yet be so close. Cordi points out some different aurora shapes her laser, "this one is called a ray, these are usually seen when the aurora is directly overhead, and this shape is an arc, this one is like a big stripe or line, and these arcs can go across the whole sky."

Seren's mam cannot contain herself any longer.

"Wow. Seren." She whispers to her daughter longingly. "You are so lucky you got to see this in real life."

"It was really so amazing..." Seren says wistfully.

Seren turns her body in the reclining seat so that her mouth is right next to her mother's ear. She wants to make sure she can hear her. What she is about to tell her is very important.

 "Mam, I want to be an aurora scientist when I grow up!"

THE END

Acknowledgements

Firstly, thanks so much to the real Dr Dan in the Space Environment Physics (SEP) group for allowing me to tag along on their expedition to Svalbard in January 2020. I learned so much about aurora physics and was totally inspired by the location, it was truly magical. All the work you do on Aurora Zoo and keeping it updated is greatly appreciated.

To the Public Engagement with Research unit without you believing in me and giving me the funding for this book it would not have happened. You folks are amazing. Thanks also to Prof Rob Fear, the head of the SEP group, for providing some extra funding to get more copies of this book printed.

To my amazing editors, 'soon to be Dr' Sam Pegg and Dr Grace O'Connor. Your edits, helpful comments, encouragement and corrections shaped this into something that now feels like an actual novel. You rule!

To my Mam, Dad, my lovely Nanny and my doggie siblings, for the inspiration, unconditional love, and support you have always shown me. To my friends, fellow astronomers and science communicators, especially my line manager, Dr Pearl John, and all the other amazing people who have inspired me over the years. I truly cannot thank you enough.

Finally, I want to thank you, the reader. You are one of the first people to read my book and that feels very special. I really hope you enjoyed reading it as much as I enjoyed writing it. I would be really very grateful if you could rate it using the QR code below. If people like the book, then I will try to get it published and on sale in actual book shops! Seren's dream is to be an aurora scientist, mine is to be a published children's author ☺

Get involved in Aurora Research

Our colleagues at the University Centre in Svalbard (UNIS) have just launched a new project called 'SolarMax' (https://www.solarmaxmission.com/) to unite Aurora Scientists, Astronauts and Citizen Scientists.

They have also made a very informative 'Aurora Handbook' and 'Field Guide' containing lots of information on how to take aurora photos and go aurora-chasing. QR code links are below:

Aurora Handbook

Aurora Field Guide

Aurora Zoo Citizen Science Project

 The University of Southampton's Space Environment Physics (SEP) group still need help analysing aurora data from their cameras in Svalbard and Tromsø, Norway.

Please help us by going to **aurorazoo.org** or scanning the QR code and clicking 'Classify'.

Learn more about climate change research in the polar regions

The National Oceanography Centre (NOC) based in Southampton is one of the partners doing important climate change research at the polar regions (in both the Artic and Antarctica).

If you would like to learn more about the work the NOC is doing go watch the video on the BIOPOLE website www.biopole.ac.uk (scroll down to the video on the home page)

Rate this book using the QR code below:

Got a Question?

Feel free to email the author, Dr Sadie Jones sadie.jones@soton.ac.uk if you have any questions about Space, the Aurora, Exoplanets, Stars, Black Holes, Planets etc. She loves answering questions about all things astronomy, and it is literally her job ☺